The Power of Invisible Chains : A Conspiracy, Crime & Political Thriller

Marcelo Palacios

Published by INDEPENDENT PUBLISHER, 2024.

This is a work of fiction. Similarities to real people, places, or events are entirely coincidental.

THE POWER OF INVISIBLE CHAINS : A CONSPIRACY, CRIME & POLITICAL THRILLER

First edition. November 20, 2024.

Copyright © 2024 Marcelo Palacios.

ISBN: 979-8227354259

Written by Marcelo Palacios.

Also by Marcelo Palacios

El Club de los Pecados Un Thriller Psicológico
La Habitación Resonante Un Thriller Psicológico
Mentiras en Código Un Thriller Político
The Political Lies A Political Thriller
Sin's Fraternity A Psychological Thriller
El Cuarto de los Ecos Un Thriller Psicologico lleno de Suspenso
The Room of Echoes A Psychological Thriller Full of Suspense
El Espejo Perturbador Un Thriller Psicologico
The Disturbing Mirror A Psychological Thriller
Luces Apagadas en la Ciudad Brillante Un Thriller Psicológico,Crimen y Policial
Lights Out in the Shining City A Psychological, Crime and Police Thriller
Under the Cloak of Horror A Criminal Psychological Thriller full of Abuse, Corruption, Mystery, Suspense and Adventure
The Housemaid's Shadow A Psychological Thriller
Unraveling Marriage, Unraveling Divorce A Domestic Thriller
The Power of Invisible Chains : A Conspiracy, Crime & Political Thriller

Table of Contents

Chapter 1: Secrets in the Smoke 1
Chapter 2: The Cartel's Reach 4
Chapter 3: Collateral Damage 7
Chapter 4: The Hidden Hand 10
Chapter 5: The Price of Loyalty 12
Chapter 6: The Labyrinth of Power 15
Chapter 7: The Political Puppet 18
Chapter 8: A Web of Betrayal 21
Chapter 9: The Death Dealer's Plot 25
Chapter 10: Crossfire in the Capitol 28
Chapter 11: Blood on the Streets 32
Chapter 12: The Cartel's Fortress 35
Chapter 13: An Unlikely Rescue 38
Chapter 14: A City Under Siege 41
Chapter 15: The Summit Gamble 44
Chapter 16: A Line in the Sand 47
Chapter 17: Against the Clock 50
Chapter 18: Collapsing Empire 53
Chapter 19: The Last Bargain 57
Chapter 20: The Chain Breaks 60

Chapter 1: Secrets in the Smoke

The aroma of freshly brewed coffee mingled with the faint scent of leather in Michael Garrett's study. A stack of unopened mail sat on the corner of his desk, but his focus remained on the digital screen in front of him. A blinking message on the encrypted terminal caught his attention, the sender's name freezing him in place: *William Lancaster*. Garrett hadn't spoken to his old mentor since leaving the military intelligence world months ago, determined to put the darkness of his past behind him.

The message was concise and chilling:

Urgent. Meet in London. A storm is coming, Michael. The kind that topples empires.

Garrett leaned back in his chair, his instincts already clawing at the calm he'd cultivated since his retirement. Lancaster wasn't one for exaggeration. The words carried the weight of an imminent threat, the kind Garrett had spent a career dismantling piece by piece.

Before he could process the implications, his phone buzzed. He answered, expecting an old friend checking in. Instead, the sharp voice of Jennifer Palmer, a State Department contact, sliced through the line.

"Michael, have you seen the news?"

"No. Why?"

"Katherine Bennett's dead. Found in Mexico City. It looks bad. You should look into it."

Katherine. Garrett's stomach tightened. They had worked together during one of his final operations, her tenacity in the field a rare quality among intelligence operatives. He barely muttered a response before hanging up.

Flipping through news reports, he found sparse details. Bennett's body had been discovered in a nondescript hotel, the cause of death ruled as a drug overdose. But the photographs of the scene—her lifeless body surrounded by scattered documents—set off alarms in Garrett's mind. Katherine didn't make careless mistakes, and she never indulged in drugs. Someone had staged the scene, but why?

The flight to London was uneventful, but Garrett's mind raced with questions. What storm was Lancaster warning about? What did Bennett uncover that cost her life? He touched down at Heathrow Airport under an overcast sky, the gray clouds mirroring the unease settling in his chest.

Lancaster chose the meeting place carefully—a centuries-old library tucked away in a quiet corner of the city. Inside, the smell of aged paper and ink was comforting, but Garrett knew this wasn't a social visit. He found Lancaster seated in a dimly lit alcove, his usual crisp suit slightly rumpled, a rare indication of stress.

"Michael," Lancaster said, standing to shake hands. His grip was firm but carried a sense of urgency.

"You've got my attention," Garrett replied, sitting across from him.

Lancaster pulled a worn leather briefcase onto the table, snapping it open to reveal a collection of files, photographs, and a single flash drive. He slid a photograph across the table—a grainy image of a man in his late forties, sharp features, and a cold intensity in his eyes.

"Ramon Ortiz," Lancaster began. "Head of an international drug cartel. Ruthless, but far more ambitious than his predecessors. He's not content with controlling narcotics; he's weaving his influence into political and economic systems worldwide."

Garrett studied the photo. "How does this tie to Katherine?"

"She was investigating a new branch of Ortiz's operations," Lancaster said. "One that merges drug trafficking with political manipulation. Her death wasn't random, Michael. Someone silenced her before she could blow the whistle."

Lancaster handed him the flash drive. "On here, you'll find encrypted files Katherine was working on. Names, accounts, movements—all tied to Ortiz. She uncovered payments to several politicians and private contractors, including firms supplying military-grade weapons."

Garrett frowned. "And you want me to pick up where she left off?"

Lancaster leaned forward, his voice lowering. "You're the only one I trust with this. Ortiz's network is vast, and his reach extends into agencies we once believed untouchable. If we don't act, this won't just destabilize governments; it'll redefine power on a global scale."

Garrett exhaled sharply. He had sworn off this life, promised himself he'd leave the cloak-and-dagger world behind. But Katherine's face haunted him. The idea of her sacrifice being buried under lies and corruption burned his resolve.

"Fine," Garrett said. "Where do we start?"

"By staying alive," Lancaster said, his gaze flicking to a nearby window.

A split second later, the glass shattered. Garrett dove instinctively, pulling Lancaster to the floor as the unmistakable crack of a rifle echoed. Dust and shards rained around them as the library patrons screamed and scattered.

Garrett pressed himself against a bookshelf, eyes scanning for the shooter's location. A second shot ripped through the air, splintering wood inches from his head. He glimpsed a glint of metal from a rooftop across the street. The sniper had a clear line of sight.

Lancaster cursed under his breath, clutching the briefcase to his chest. "We've been made."

"No kidding," Garrett snapped, pulling his sidearm. He motioned for Lancaster to stay low as he crept toward an emergency exit. Another shot rang out, this one striking a nearby lamp, plunging the alcove into flickering shadows.

Garrett kicked the door open, ushering Lancaster into the alley behind the library. The two ran, weaving through narrow streets as the sound of pursuing footsteps grew closer. Whoever was after them wasn't just a hired gun; their precision and coordination suggested a well-trained operative.

They rounded a corner, only to find themselves blocked by a black SUV screeching to a halt. The passenger door opened, revealing a man in tactical gear armed with an assault rifle.

Chapter 2: The Cartel's Reach

The SUV roared down the alley as Garrett yanked Lancaster out of its path. Bullets ricocheted off brick and steel as Garrett fired back, hitting one of the tires. The vehicle swerved, smashing into a dumpster before the gunman inside could recover. Garrett and Lancaster bolted into the maze of streets, their breath ragged, adrenaline pumping as the pursuit faded into the distance.

Hours later, Garrett sat in a dimly lit apartment in London, the flash drive Lancaster had given him plugged into a secured laptop. The files were heavily encrypted, layers of code shielding the details Katherine had died for. Garrett's fingers moved with precision, bypassing some of the simpler barriers, but even with his skills, the decryption would take time.

Lancaster poured two glasses of whiskey. "You need help cracking that."

"I know someone," Garrett replied without looking up. "But first, tell me more about this connection to the pharmaceutical world."

Lancaster leaned against the window, swirling his drink. "Ortiz isn't just smuggling drugs. He's funneling funds through dummy corporations, one of which is tied to BioGenTech Pharmaceuticals. A subsidiary there appears to be developing synthetic opioids—stronger, cheaper, and far deadlier."

"Legal distribution covering an illegal trade," Garrett muttered, piecing it together.

The laptop chimed, signaling partial access to the files. Scanning the decrypted portion, Garrett found transaction records and emails that hinted at direct communication between Ortiz's cartel and executives within BioGenTech. Names and dates blurred together, but one name caught his eye: *Thomas Greene*.

"Thomas Greene," Garrett said, leaning back. "BioGenTech's COO. He's been attending trade expos in Mexico City."

Lancaster nodded. "That lines up. If he's working with Ortiz, Mexico City is the hub for their operations. You'll need someone on the ground there."

Within twenty-four hours, Garrett was en route to Mexico City. The bustling streets were a sharp contrast to the murky world he was diving back into. His contact, Diego Ramirez, waited for him at a crowded café, the air thick with the aroma of fresh tortillas and coffee.

Ramirez was younger than Garrett expected, his clean-shaven face marked by sharp determination. He extended a hand. "Michael Garrett. I've heard a lot about you."

"Hope it's the good stuff," Garrett replied, taking the seat opposite him.

The conversation was brisk, professional. Ramirez had been tracking Ortiz's cartel for years, watching it evolve from a drug-smuggling operation to an enterprise with political and corporate influence.

"They've moved beyond drugs," Ramirez explained, spreading photographs across the table. "Smuggling weapons, laundering money through tech startups, and now, pharmaceuticals. The warehouse we're about to visit isn't just a depot. It's a nerve center for their operations in the city."

Night fell as Garrett and Ramirez approached the industrial district. The warehouse loomed ahead, its rusted exterior and overgrown weeds a façade for the dangerous secrets within. Garrett's military training kicked in, every sound and shadow analyzed as they crept toward the entrance. Ramirez produced a set of bolt cutters, quickly dismantling the padlock on a side door.

Inside, the warehouse was a cavernous expanse filled with crates, pallets, and dimly lit corridors. The faint hum of machinery buzzed in the background, accompanied by the distant murmur of voices. Garrett's eyes scanned the space, noting the markings on several crates—logos of BioGenTech alongside military-grade serial numbers.

"This is bigger than I thought," Ramirez whispered, his flashlight beam catching a stack of documents on a nearby table. Garrett flipped through the pages, finding shipping manifests that confirmed weapons were being funneled to multiple regions under the guise of agricultural equipment.

Footsteps echoed in the distance. Garrett motioned for Ramirez to stay low as they moved deeper into the labyrinth. At the heart of the warehouse, they stumbled upon a small conference room. Through the cracked blinds, Garrett saw a group of men in heated discussion.

Ramon Ortiz sat at the head of the table, his sharp features illuminated by the harsh light overhead. Beside him was a man Garrett immediately recognized from the files: Thomas Greene. The BioGenTech executive spoke with a cold confidence, gesturing toward a map of global shipping routes pinned to the wall.

Garrett's pulse quickened as he listened in. Greene was outlining a plan to expand their synthetic opioid distribution into Europe, using diplomatic shipments as cover. Ortiz nodded approvingly, adding a chilling reminder about eliminating any obstacles.

Ramirez tapped Garrett's shoulder, motioning toward an unguarded stack of files near the room's entrance. They moved silently, gathering as many documents as they could carry, but a sudden noise made Garrett freeze.

A steel pipe clattered to the ground behind them. Garrett spun around, locking eyes with a cartel enforcer armed with an assault rifle.

Chapter 3: Collateral Damage

The enforcer's shout shattered the silence, and chaos erupted. Garrett shoved Ramirez to the ground as a barrage of gunfire tore through the air. Sparks flew as bullets struck metal crates, and alarms blared through the warehouse. Garrett ducked behind a steel pillar, his pistol snapping off calculated shots.

"Back exit!" Ramirez yelled, gesturing toward a shadowy corridor.

Garrett laid down suppressive fire, hitting one of the enforcers in the shoulder, while Ramirez sprinted toward the passage. More cartel reinforcements spilled into the warehouse, their weapons blazing. Garrett cursed under his breath, his mind racing as he retreated toward Ramirez's position.

"Go, go!" Ramirez urged as Garrett reached him, and they both bolted through the maze of corridors. The thundering footsteps of their pursuers closed in, but Garrett spotted a service ladder leading to a catwalk. He motioned for Ramirez to climb.

From the elevated vantage point, Garrett fired down at the advancing gunmen. The high ground gave them a slim advantage, but the cartel operatives spread out, flanking them. A bullet grazed Garrett's arm, the sharp pain jolting him. He gritted his teeth, focusing on their escape.

At the far end of the catwalk, a large skylight offered a risky but viable exit. Ramirez grabbed a crowbar from a nearby tool rack and smashed the glass. The shards rained down as they leapt through, landing hard on a truck parked below.

The duo hit the ground running, weaving through the rows of parked vehicles in the lot outside. Garrett heard the roar of engines as their pursuers gave chase.

"We need to split up!" Garrett said, shoving a bundle of stolen documents into Ramirez's hands. "Take this and meet me at the safe house. I'll draw them off!"

Ramirez hesitated for a moment before nodding and disappearing into the night. Garrett darted in the opposite direction, his every step calculated to mislead their hunters. He eventually slipped into the shadows of a nearby alley and vanished into the sprawling chaos of Mexico City.

Hours later, they reconvened at a safe house on the outskirts of the city. Ramirez's face was pale, his hands trembling as he spread the stolen documents across a table. Garrett scanned the pages, his eyes narrowing at the detailed records of payments flowing from Ortiz's cartel to an anonymous political entity labeled only as "Sentinel."

"This isn't just corruption," Ramirez said, his voice low. "These payments are massive. Someone in Washington is not just complicit—they're orchestrating something big."

Garrett's stomach tightened as he flipped through the ledger. Among the usual cartel expenses—bribes, weapons, and logistics—were alarming entries referencing military-grade technology shipments. Serial numbers and specs stood out like a neon warning sign.

"This is classified tech," Garrett said grimly. "Hardware that shouldn't leave U.S. soil, let alone end up in cartel hands."

Before they could delve further, Garrett's phone buzzed. The secure line connected him to Lancaster, who wasted no time. "I've seen some of the data you transmitted," Lancaster said. "If you think Ortiz's cartel is the only enemy, you're gravely mistaken. These players are entrenched. Every step you take will expose you to retaliation. Tread carefully, Michael."

"We don't have the luxury of caution," Garrett replied. "Ramirez and I have a lead—a political connection that could blow this wide open."

Lancaster sighed heavily. "Just remember, the deeper you dig, the harder it will be to get out alive."

The call ended, but Lancaster's words lingered as Garrett considered their next move. Ramirez pulled out his laptop, beginning the process of analyzing the data further. Meanwhile, Garrett contacted Jennifer Palmer, a U.S. diplomat stationed in Mexico City. Her reputation as a shrewd operator preceded her, and Garrett hoped she could shed light on the political angle.

Palmer met them in a nondescript café the next morning, her demeanor composed but wary. She sat across from Garrett and Ramirez, her sharp eyes scanning the room before leaning in.

"What you're uncovering is bigger than you realize," Palmer said softly. "Ortiz's network isn't just about drugs and weapons. There are people in positions of power—politicians, executives—who see his cartel as a tool. They're using him to destabilize regions and consolidate control."

Garrett pressed her for specifics, but Palmer hesitated. "I can't name names. Not yet. But I'll say this: one of Ortiz's allies has close ties to a high-ranking official in Washington. Someone who could bury your investigation before it even gains traction."

Palmer handed Garrett a slip of paper with a single word: "Catalyst." She offered no explanation but promised to arrange another meeting soon.

As they left the café, Ramirez received a text message on his phone. The screen glowed with a single line of text: *We know where your family is. Stay out of this.*

Chapter 4: The Hidden Hand

Jennifer Palmer's expression was grave as she leaned forward in the dimly lit café. The hum of voices around them was a shield, but Garrett could feel her unease.

"Katherine wasn't just in the wrong place at the wrong time," Palmer began, her voice low but steady. "Her murder was an inside job. Someone on our side silenced her before she could blow the whistle on Ortiz's operations. Whatever she uncovered was big enough to make her a target."

Ramirez clenched his fists, his eyes darting toward Garrett, who remained stone-faced. Garrett finally broke the silence. "Do you have proof?"

Palmer shook her head. "No hard proof, but I've heard whispers. Katherine had documents—names, transactions, everything. But those files disappeared when she died."

Garrett exchanged a glance with Ramirez, their unspoken agreement clear. They needed to follow the trail Katherine had started.

The ledger became their guide. Among the coded transactions and offshore accounts was a key entry pointing to a financial institution in London—a well-known bank with a history of discreet dealings. Garrett and Ramirez knew they needed Lancaster's expertise to crack the next layer of the conspiracy.

Two days later, the three of them convened in a safe house on the outskirts of London. Lancaster, calm and calculating as ever, spread blueprints of the bank across a table. "This institution has been laundering money for Ortiz's network for years," he explained. "Their encryption is military-grade, but I've arranged for access to their internal systems. You'll have about ten minutes before they notice the breach."

"That's all we need," Garrett replied.

The plan was straightforward but perilous. Lancaster would distract the bank's personnel with a fabricated emergency while Garrett infiltrated the server room. Ramirez would monitor the operation from a van parked nearby, prepared to extract them if things went south.

The operation began smoothly. Lancaster, posing as an eccentric investor, marched into the bank's lobby, waving fabricated credentials and demanding an urgent meeting with the manager. His charisma and apparent importance bought Garrett the time he needed to slip past the security desk.

In the basement, the hum of servers filled the narrow, fluorescent-lit room. Garrett quickly plugged a modified USB drive into the main terminal and began extracting data. As lines of code streamed across the screen, his heart raced. The system's defenses were formidable, but Lancaster's access codes worked like a charm.

Ramirez's voice crackled through the earpiece. "You've got five minutes. How's it looking?"

"Close," Garrett muttered, his fingers flying over the keyboard. "I'm pulling massive transaction logs. This isn't just cartel money—it's tied to a pharmaceutical executive back in the States. Thomas Greene."

Ramirez's sharp intake of breath was audible. "Greene? The guy's a poster child for corporate America."

Garrett's screen flashed green. "Got it," he said. "I'm wiping my trail and—"

The terminal locked suddenly, and a red warning appeared: *Unauthorized Access Detected.*

Above, in the lobby, Lancaster's fabricated crisis unraveled as alarms blared throughout the building. The calm, professional atmosphere of the bank erupted into chaos. Security guards exchanged tense words over their radios before fanning out toward the exits.

Ramirez's voice came through again, more urgent this time. "You've got company, Garrett. Get out of there now!"

Lancaster, still holding his ground in the lobby, gave Garrett precious seconds by escalating his faux meltdown. "You call this service?" he shouted, pounding a fist on the manager's desk. "This is an outrage!"

Meanwhile, Garrett unplugged his drive, shoving it into his jacket pocket before darting toward the stairwell. His shoes echoed on the cold metal steps as he ascended, but the heavy footsteps of guards in pursuit grew louder.

He burst into the lobby just as Lancaster's theatrics reached their peak. Garrett grabbed Lancaster by the arm. "Time to go."

Lancaster nodded, dropping his act instantly. Together, they pushed through the crowded lobby toward the exit. Behind them, the guards yelled, their radios buzzing with commands.

As they reached the glass doors leading to the street, the alarms shifted to a shriller tone. Garrett glanced back and spotted a team of armed responders converging on their location.

Chapter 5: The Price of Loyalty

Garrett and Lancaster sprinted down the rain-slick London streets, the wail of alarms still echoing from the bank they had just infiltrated. Traffic blurred into streaks of red and white as the two men weaved through pedestrians, their breaths coming in sharp bursts. Behind them, the pounding steps of the bank's guards gave way to the heavier sound of car engines revving to life.

Around the corner, a nondescript sedan idled, Ramirez at the wheel. "Get in!" he barked.

Garrett yanked open the door, shoving Lancaster inside before diving in himself. The car peeled out, tires screeching, narrowly avoiding an oncoming taxi. Lancaster glanced back at the shrinking figures of armed pursuers, his expression grim but composed.

"That was closer than I'd have liked," Lancaster muttered, straightening his tie as though they'd just left a tense meeting rather than a high-stakes heist.

Garrett ignored the remark, pulling out the USB drive. "We got what we came for, but they know we're on to them now. Ramirez, step on it. If Greene's people are half as ruthless as I think, this isn't over."

The words proved prophetic. Moments later, a sleek black SUV appeared in the rearview mirror, its headlights cutting through the foggy night. Ramirez cursed under his breath and floored the accelerator.

The ensuing chase was a violent ballet of screeching brakes and sharp turns. Garrett leaned out the window, aiming a compact pistol at the pursuing vehicle. A shot rang out, shattering one of the SUV's headlights, but it didn't slow.

"They're not backing off!" Ramirez shouted, swerving to avoid a delivery truck.

Lancaster gripped the edge of his seat, his usual composure slipping. "Drive faster, or they'll box us in!"

A narrow alley appeared on the left, and Ramirez didn't hesitate, veering sharply. The sedan scraped against the walls, sparks flying as it forced its way through. The SUV hesitated, unable to follow. For the moment, they were free.

When they reached a safe house on the outskirts of the city, Garrett wasted no time plugging the USB into a secure laptop. The files painted a damning picture. Greene's corporation wasn't just laundering money for Ortiz's cartel—it was funding a secret lab in Bogota. The lab specialized in bioengineered narcotics designed to hook users more effectively while offering strategic leverage over rival cartels and even governments.

"This isn't just drugs," Garrett said, his voice tight. "It's control. They're manufacturing dependency on a global scale."

Lancaster nodded, his expression unreadable. "It's not surprising. Greene's ambition has always been matched by his lack of scruples. But this..." He gestured to the screen, where detailed schematics of the lab and its distribution network glowed ominously. "This changes the game."

Meanwhile, back in Mexico City, Ramirez had more immediate concerns. He sat in a dimly lit office at the Federal Police headquarters, scanning through files on Ortiz's known associates. The room felt heavier than usual, the tension in the air palpable.

He barely noticed when his colleague, Lieutenant Marquez, entered. "Diego," Marquez said, his tone oddly flat. "Can I have a word?"

Ramirez gestured for him to sit, but before he could say another word, Marquez drew a pistol and aimed it directly at Ramirez's chest.

"What the hell is this?" Ramirez demanded, his chair scraping the floor as he stood.

Marquez's face betrayed no emotion. "You've gone too far. Ortiz knows everything. Your family won't be safe unless you stop now."

The two men stared each other down, the room charged with deadly intent. Before Marquez could pull the trigger, Ramirez lunged, grabbing the barrel of the gun and twisting it away. The shot went wide, shattering a framed photograph on the wall.

A brief but brutal struggle ended with Ramirez pinning Marquez to the floor, disarming him. The realization that even his closest colleagues couldn't be trusted hit him harder than the fight itself.

Hours later, Ramirez sat in the safe house he shared with his wife, Sofia, and their young daughter. He hadn't told them about the confrontation, but the tension in his shoulders gave away that something was wrong. Sofia handed him a cup of coffee, her concerned eyes searching his.

Before he could offer reassurance, a blinding flash lit up the street outside, followed by a deafening explosion. The force of the blast shattered the windows, throwing Ramirez and Sofia to the ground.

14

When the ringing in his ears subsided, Ramirez scrambled to his feet, shouting Sofia's name. She lay a few feet away, dazed but conscious. Blood trickled from a cut on her forehead.

Chapter 6: The Labyrinth of Power

The heavy rain slashed against the windows of the military-grade vehicle as it rumbled through the winding streets of Bogota. The city's skyline blurred into the distance, shrouded by thick clouds, while Garrett and Ramirez remained silent, each man lost in his thoughts. The mission at hand was like a tightrope walk, where one misstep could send them plummeting into a deeper abyss.

"Ready?" Ramirez's voice broke the stillness. He glanced at Garrett, eyes steely with determination.

Garrett nodded, but there was an unmistakable edge to his expression. "As ready as I'll ever be."

They arrived at a nondescript industrial complex on the outskirts of the city, an imposing structure surrounded by high fences and tight security. It was an old warehouse, easily overlooked by anyone unfamiliar with the area. But Garrett and Ramirez knew better. This was Greene's secret lab, where the cartel was producing more than just drugs.

The two men exited the vehicle, each carrying an array of tools designed to help them breach the heavily guarded facility. Garrett adjusted his tactical vest, making sure his equipment was secure. Ramirez, ever the professional, didn't speak but checked his sidearm before leading the way toward a service entrance, hidden from the guards' line of sight.

Inside, the lab was a grim sight. The sterile white walls and the humming of machines gave off a cold, clinical feel, but what struck Garrett the most were the cages. Rows upon rows of locked metal cells lined the walls, each one containing emaciated, terrified subjects. Their eyes were vacant, as if their souls had been drained. Some were barely conscious, others were twitching uncontrollably, their bodies writhing from the effects of the cruel experiments they were subjected to.

"This is worse than I imagined," Garrett muttered, his voice barely above a whisper.

Ramirez's face tightened, his fists clenched. "Ortiz's reach is everywhere. But Greene... this is beyond anything I've ever seen."

The pair moved quickly through the facility, following the narrow, dimly lit corridors that seemed to spiral deeper into the heart of the operation. They avoided detection by ducking into shadows, slipping past patrolling guards, and using their intimate knowledge of military tactics to stay out of sight.

Eventually, they found themselves in a high-security lab. The room was filled with rows of monitors displaying real-time data on the test subjects, as well as maps of cartel territories. There, Garrett found what they were looking for: files on Greene's partnership with Ramon Ortiz.

Greene wasn't just helping Ortiz launder money or supply drugs—he was developing a new kind of narcotic, one that would allow Ortiz to control a private army of soldiers. The drug, still in its early stages, was designed to increase aggression, reduce fear, and enhance physical performance, turning ordinary men into lethal killing machines.

Garrett's mind raced as he downloaded the files, knowing that the data they had obtained could be the key to unraveling Ortiz's entire operation. He moved to the exit, but just as he reached the door, the sharp sound of footsteps echoed down the hall.

"Shit," Ramirez muttered, his eyes scanning the room for an escape route.

Before Garrett could react, the lab's security doors slammed shut, locking them inside. A cold, mechanical voice echoed through the speakers: "Intruders detected. Security breach in progress."

Garrett's heart pounded in his chest. They had triggered the alarm. It was only a matter of time before the cartel's hitmen descended on them.

Ramirez grabbed Garrett by the arm. "This way." He pulled Garrett through a narrow vent shaft, the air thick with the scent of chemicals. They crawled through the tight space, their bodies pressed against the cold metal walls.

After what felt like an eternity, they emerged into a dimly lit maintenance corridor. Ramirez quickly scanned the hallway, motioning for Garrett to follow. But as they turned the corner, they came face-to-face with a group of cartel enforcers, heavily armed and clearly anticipating their arrival.

The hitmen raised their weapons, their eyes gleaming with deadly intent. Garrett and Ramirez took cover behind a series of crates, returning fire as the men began to advance. The sound of gunfire echoed through the corridors, the chaos intensifying with each passing second.

Garrett's mind raced. They couldn't hold off this many for long. He grabbed Ramirez by the shoulder. "We need to get to the roof. Now!"

Ramirez didn't hesitate, leading the way as the two men fought their way through the compound. They reached a stairwell and began climbing, their hearts pounding in their chests.

But just as they reached the rooftop, they were met with an unexpected challenge. Standing at the top of the stairs, blocking their escape, was a lone hitman. His face was hidden behind a high-tech helmet, and his body was clad in advanced military armor. He wasn't just any enforcer—this was someone from the inner circle of the cartel, a man trained to kill with ruthless efficiency.

The hitman raised a futuristic assault rifle, his movements smooth and calculated. Garrett and Ramirez were cornered. There was no way out.

The air crackled with tension as the hitman took a step forward, his gun aimed directly at Garrett. A smirk played at the corner of his lips, as if he knew that in this moment, victory was assured.

Chapter 7: The Political Puppet

The tension in the room was palpable as Garrett sat across from Jennifer Palmer in her sparse office near the heart of Washington, D.C. A large map of the United States and international political connections hung behind her, marking various key locations with pins of different colors. The afternoon sunlight filtered through the blinds, casting long shadows across the floor, yet neither of them paid attention to the hour. They were focused solely on the task at hand.

Jennifer's fingers tapped nervously on the surface of her desk. "The evidence is irrefutable," she said, her voice low but firm. "Greene isn't just working with Ortiz. He's in bed with Senator Gregory Milton. The senator is getting kickbacks from the cartel, funds routed through a series of offshore accounts, likely hidden behind shell companies."

Garrett's eyes narrowed as he studied the document in front of him. He didn't flinch. "Milton. I should have suspected him. He's always been the type to play both sides. But this... this is something else."

Jennifer nodded grimly. "And it gets worse. From what I can gather, Milton has used his influence to shield Ortiz's operations in exchange for campaign donations and, most likely, promises of protection. Ortiz's network of power has already infiltrated several levels of the government. If we expose this, it could unravel everything."

Garrett's hand hovered over the document, then slammed it down onto the desk. "We can't back down now. We've come too far."

Jennifer leaned back in her chair, her gaze fixed on Garrett. "You're right. But exposing Milton means confronting the entire structure of political corruption that Ortiz has built. It won't just end with him. It's a whole network."

Garrett stood up, a sense of urgency mounting in his chest. "Then we need to get to him. If Milton falls, maybe we can bring down the whole operation. We need leverage."

Jennifer smiled faintly, but it was more of a grim acknowledgment. "That's where you're wrong. Milton's power runs much deeper than we thought. He's not just a pawn in this. He's one of the key players. If we try to move on him directly, he'll crush us."

Garrett's eyes darkened as he considered her words. He had no illusions about the political machine they were dealing with. He had seen firsthand how corruption could thrive under layers of bureaucracy, like a parasitic growth hidden in plain sight. But something had changed in him since Katherine's death. It wasn't just the mission anymore. It was personal.

He left Jennifer's office in a daze, his mind racing with strategies, dangers, and the heavy weight of responsibility. He needed to act fast, but this time, the stakes were even higher. Senator Milton wasn't just another corrupt politician. He was connected to a transnational criminal empire with access to military-grade technology, mercenaries, and the sort of influence that could destroy entire governments.

Meanwhile, in Mexico, Ramirez was preparing to take a trip back to his home country. Garrett had insisted he stay in the United States for safety, but Ramirez's primary concern was his family. He knew the cartel would retaliate soon, and the message left on his phone was clear. Ortiz knew where they lived.

Ramirez had been given a temporary safe house in the U.S., but his heart was in Mexico. He needed to secure his family before they became collateral damage.

"Be careful," Garrett had warned him, his voice tense with concern. "Ortiz won't stop until he's secured everything. And the worst part is, you're one of the few people who knows how deep this runs. You're a target now, too."

"I know." Ramirez's expression had hardened. "But I'll do whatever it takes to keep them safe. I'm not going to let them be part of this war."

As Garrett's mind wandered to the logistics of taking down Milton, Lancaster had been working in the background, tracing Ortiz's financial empire. Using a network of offshore accounts, Lancaster had discovered a series of shell companies linked directly to Greene. The money laundering was far-reaching, touching on military contracts, foreign investments, and a staggering amount of illicit funds being funneled through various banks in Europe and the Caribbean.

The deeper Lancaster dug, the more complex the operation appeared. Each company on the surface seemed legitimate, yet each had connections leading straight back to Ortiz. If Garrett and Lancaster wanted to bring down this house of cards, they would need to expose every single one of these entities. And that was where the real danger lay.

Garrett knew he had to confront Milton—head-on. But he wasn't foolish enough to walk into the lion's den without a plan. He needed to get close, to hear what the senator was saying in private. With the help of Jennifer's resources, Garrett had arranged for a covert surveillance operation.

It was a risky move. Milton's office was heavily guarded, and the senator was known to have connections in high places. If they moved too soon, they would blow their cover, and the entire operation would fall apart.

Garrett waited in the shadows outside Milton's office, a pair of binoculars in hand. He had infiltrated the building under the guise of a political donor, using his connections with a few key figures in Washington. The senator's office was located in one of the city's most secure government buildings, nestled among the towering stone facades of the Capitol.

As the sun dipped below the horizon, Garrett slipped into the building's parking garage and made his way toward Milton's office. He couldn't afford to make any mistakes.

He reached the office undetected, his heart beating in his chest. He tapped into the bugging system with precision, making sure the microphones were in place. He needed to hear what Milton was planning, needed to understand his next move.

Minutes passed. The voices on the other side of the door began to grow louder. Garrett settled into the shadows, listening intently as the conversation took shape. What he overheard would change everything.

"We can't afford to let Garrett get any closer," Milton's voice came through clearly. "If he digs any deeper, everything's going to collapse. We need to eliminate him—quietly. No trace. He's becoming a liability."

Garrett froze. The walls seemed to close in around him as he processed what he had just heard. The threat was real. The senator had just signed his own death sentence.

But Garrett's next move was uncertain. Milton's web of influence had just expanded far beyond anything he had imagined. It wasn't just about taking down a politician anymore. It was about staying alive long enough to expose everything.

Chapter 8: A Web of Betrayal

The night was warm as Garrett stood just outside the entrance to the high-profile gala, surveying the crowd that gathered in the grand ballroom. The event, hosted by a prominent lobbyist with ties to various powerful politicians, was the perfect cover for his infiltration. People in expensive suits and evening gowns drifted past him, laughing and engaging in polite conversation, unaware of the dangerous game being played behind the scenes.

Garrett adjusted his suit jacket, ensuring the concealed earpiece was firmly in place. As a security consultant, he had access to the event's inner workings, which would give him the perfect excuse to move freely throughout the venue. His role was simple—watch, listen, and gather the information needed to bring down Senator Milton and his associates.

He had to keep his focus. The gala wasn't just a lavish social event; it was a front for a secretive meeting between Milton, Thomas Greene, and Robert Kendrick. Garrett had learned that Kendrick, an international arms dealer with long-standing ties to Ortiz, was the missing link in the cartel's operations. The arms shipments that fueled the cartel's private army came from Kendrick's network, a vast underground empire that spanned the globe.

Garrett had a plan—he would get close to the group, gain their trust, and record everything. But the risk was enormous. If he were caught, there was no telling what would happen. Kendrick was notorious for his brutal methods of dealing with anyone who posed a threat to his business.

He entered the ballroom, blending seamlessly into the crowd. The walls were adorned with portraits of influential figures, and soft classical music played in the background, adding an air of elegance. The light from crystal chandeliers bounced off polished marble floors, creating an atmosphere of excess and wealth. But beneath this façade, Garrett knew the true nature of the gathering.

His eyes scanned the room until they landed on Milton, who was deep in conversation with Thomas Greene. The two men were standing near the bar, their voices low but clearly animated. Garrett's pulse quickened when he noticed Kendrick leaning against the far wall, his sharp eyes watching the crowd. Kendrick was every bit the ruthless arms dealer Garrett had expected—his presence alone commanded respect, his reputation for violence well-earned.

22

Garrett adjusted his position, keeping a few steps away from the group. He casually sipped from his champagne flute as he moved closer, just within earshot. He could hear snippets of their conversation, though it was impossible to make out the full details. Milton's hand was waving in the air, as if he was trying to explain something. Greene nodded with a smug expression, while Kendrick remained silent, his gaze piercing the room.

Garrett approached quietly, ensuring his movements were fluid. He activated the discreet recorder hidden inside the cufflink of his sleeve. His eyes locked onto the group, keeping careful track of every movement. This was his chance to gather irrefutable evidence of the cartel's connections to the government and the international arms trade. He had to get close, but not too close. He couldn't afford to blow his cover.

As the conversation between the men grew more heated, Garrett's focus sharpened. Milton was speaking about an upcoming vote on military spending, something that would have major implications for the arms trade. Greene and Kendrick were discussing a large shipment of military-grade weapons that was scheduled to arrive from Eastern Europe. Garrett's instincts told him that this was no ordinary shipment—it was likely part of a larger deal involving the cartel's private army.

"Milton, we need this vote in our favor," Greene said, his voice low and insistent. "If you can't deliver, I'll have to reconsider our deal. Ortiz isn't going to wait forever. He expects results."

Milton's expression tightened, but he quickly regained his composure. "You'll have your vote. The bill will pass. But I need something in return. I want guarantees on the protection of my interests. This isn't just about guns. I've got enemies closing in."

Kendrick finally spoke up, his voice calm but tinged with menace. "We all have enemies, Milton. That's why we're here—because we can protect each other. But you need to remember one thing. If you fail us now, there will be consequences."

Garrett's pulse quickened as the pieces of the puzzle fell into place. The cartel wasn't just fueling its army with drugs and cash—it was building an entire geopolitical strategy, and Milton was a key player in that plan. His political influence and the support of people like Greene and Kendrick gave the cartel the power it needed to control governments and military forces.

Suddenly, Kendrick's sharp gaze flicked toward Garrett, and Garrett felt a cold shiver run down his spine. There was no mistaking the suspicion in the arms dealer's eyes. The way Kendrick was looking at him made Garrett's heart race. Had he been spotted?

He tried to remain calm, carefully maintaining his position in the crowd. He didn't want to draw any attention to himself, but it was clear that Kendrick was becoming increasingly aware of his presence. The arms dealer's lips curled into a tight smile as he made his way toward Garrett.

"Do you work here?" Kendrick asked, his voice smooth but edged with a quiet threat.

Garrett swallowed hard, forcing a smile as he turned to face the man. "Yes, sir. I'm a security consultant. Just making sure everything is in order."

Kendrick's eyes narrowed slightly. "Funny. I don't remember seeing you before. Are you sure you're in the right place?"

Garrett nodded quickly, trying to mask his growing anxiety. "Of course, sir. I've been with the event staff all evening."

Kendrick's gaze lingered for a moment longer before he nodded slowly, his expression unreadable. "Well, don't let me keep you."

Garrett backed away slowly, his heart pounding in his chest. He had narrowly avoided suspicion—but Kendrick was smart. He knew something was off. Garrett's cover was close to being blown, and the danger was closing in. He needed to get out of there before Kendrick decided to act on his suspicions.

Just as he was about to make his exit, a voice crackled through his earpiece.

"Garrett, it's Jennifer. Get out of there now. Kendrick's guards are moving toward you."

Garrett's eyes darted toward Kendrick, who was now signaling to his men. The guards were closing in, and Garrett realized that his time was running out.

He turned quickly and made his way toward the exit, his mind racing. He had the evidence he needed. But it wasn't enough to stop what was coming. Kendrick's guards were already following him, and Garrett could feel the weight of the impending danger.

The doors to the ballroom opened just as Garrett stepped into the hallway, and he sprinted toward the back exit. The sound of footsteps grew louder behind him, and he knew that Kendrick's men were only moments away from catching up.

With each step, the pressure mounted. There was no escape.

Chapter 9: The Death Dealer's Plot

Garrett's heart raced as he dashed through the narrow alleyways, his breath coming in short, ragged bursts. Kendrick's guards were closing in, and the noise of their pursuit echoed behind him. His mind was racing, calculating his next move as he turned a sharp corner and leapt over a chain-link fence. He could hear footsteps getting closer. They were on his tail, and they wouldn't stop until they had him.

The city was a maze of buildings, each one offering a potential escape route, but Garrett had to think fast. He was running on instinct now, adrenaline fueling his every movement. The sound of heavy boots pounding the pavement grew louder. He glanced over his shoulder for a split second—four of Kendrick's men, all armed and closing in fast. They were professional. No one would be able to survive if they caught him in a place like this.

He turned another corner and spotted a fire escape ladder hanging off the side of a nearby building. Without thinking, he sprinted toward it, grabbing the cold metal rungs with urgency. His fingers slipped once or twice, but he didn't have time to care. His body was a blur as he climbed, pulling himself up as fast as he could. The roar of his pursuers grew quieter, but he knew it wasn't over. Not yet.

Once at the top, Garrett rolled over the edge of the roof and onto solid ground. He crouched low, listening carefully. The rooftop was littered with old vents, rusty HVAC units, and forgotten crates. A perfect place to hide... for a moment. He didn't plan on staying long.

Below him, he could hear the sound of the guards' footsteps as they raced up the stairs, shouting orders to each other. "Split up! He can't have gone far!"

Garrett's mind was a whirlwind. He had to get out of the city. He had to meet with Palmer and share his findings before it was too late. But first, he had to make sure Kendrick's men weren't going to catch him. He crept to the edge of the roof and peered over, watching the guards carefully as they scanned the alley below.

He held his breath, praying they wouldn't look up. His luck seemed to hold for a moment longer, but that fragile peace shattered when one of the guards raised his head. His eyes locked with Garrett's, just for a second, before Garrett turned and bolted for the other side of the roof.

The chase was back on.

Garrett leapt over a series of low walls, his legs pumping as he ran. The city stretched out before him, a maze of rooftops, alleys, and streets. He was trying to think ahead, calculating his route to avoid getting cornered. If he could make it to the next building, he'd be able to swing across the alley using the fire escape. That was his plan, but the guards were relentless. He could hear their shouts growing louder, echoing off the surrounding buildings.

He reached the next roof and barely made it over the edge before a bullet whizzed past his ear. The force of it made his heart skip a beat. He ducked behind an old water tower just in time as another shot rang out, hitting the metal behind him. The sound of the gunshot rattled him, but he didn't have the luxury of panic. He was running out of time.

Garrett kept moving, staying low as he maneuvered from one rooftop to the next. His mind was focused on only one thing: escape. He couldn't afford to be caught, not when he had so much information to pass on. His findings were too important.

After what felt like hours of zigzagging through the city, Garrett finally reached the edge of a building that faced a narrow street. He dropped down onto the fire escape ladder and carefully descended to the ground, making sure to keep a low profile. He darted across the street and into a series of alleyways, winding his way through the dark, deserted paths until he reached his destination.

His breath came in heavy gasps, and the cold air bit at his skin, but Garrett was relieved to have escaped. He ducked into an unmarked van, parked in a dark corner. Palmer was already waiting inside, her expression tense as she looked up from her phone.

"Garrett, you okay?" she asked quietly.

"I'm fine," Garrett replied, still panting. "But we need to talk. I've got the evidence we need."

He handed Palmer a small encrypted drive, containing the recordings from the gala, as well as the data he had pulled from Kendrick and Greene. Palmer's eyes flicked over the files quickly, her face grim as she processed the information.

"This is huge, Garrett," she said, her voice low. "Milton's compromised. Greene's operations are bigger than we thought. And Kendrick—this arms deal with Ortiz... it's massive."

"I know," Garrett muttered, feeling the weight of the situation. "But there's more. Kendrick's men are after me. We're running out of time. I need you to set up a meeting with your CIA contacts. We need to bring this to them before Kendrick does something worse."

Palmer nodded, already tapping on her phone to arrange a covert meeting. "I'll get this information to the right people. We'll have to move quickly, though. This thing's snowballing."

Garrett sat back, exhausted but relieved that Palmer had his back. But his moment of relief was short-lived. A voice suddenly crackled through his earpiece, coming from Lancaster.

"Garrett, I've got something," Lancaster's voice was sharp. "Ortiz is planning a large-scale smuggling operation using diplomatic immunity to bypass borders. He's using government connections to move military-grade tech across multiple countries. This is bigger than we thought."

Garrett's blood ran cold. Diplomatic immunity—if Ortiz was pulling this off, it meant the cartel had infiltrated not only military circles but also government offices. They were in too deep.

"We need to shut this down before it gets worse," Garrett said, looking at Palmer. "Let's meet with the CIA. I'll brief them, but we need to move fast."

As Palmer nodded and typed a message, Garrett felt a wave of dread wash over him. The pieces were falling into place, and the gravity of the situation was finally sinking in. They were up against an enemy that had infiltrated the highest levels of power. And soon, they would face the consequences of their actions.

As they drove away from the rendezvous point, Garrett felt his phone buzz. When he checked it, his stomach dropped.

His apartment had been ransacked.

A single message was left behind: "Stay out, or die."

The implications were clear. They knew he was coming for them. And they weren't playing games anymore.

Chapter 10: Crossfire in the Capitol

The Capitol was buzzing with anticipation. News outlets were already stationed along the corridors, cameras flashing, eager to capture every moment of the press conference that Senator Gregory Milton had called. The stakes had never been higher. Milton had been under intense scrutiny for his ties to the Ortiz cartel, and Garrett and Palmer were about to push him further into the corner.

Garrett sat in the back of the room, just behind a row of reporters, his fingers wrapped around the cold handle of his coffee mug. Palmer was seated beside him, her eyes scanning the crowd with sharp precision. They had done everything in their power to make sure today's meeting would be a turning point. The information they had gathered from Kendrick, Greene, and the others—Milton's involvement in the cartel's smuggling network—was about to be exposed.

The plan was simple: intercept one of the cartel's shipments, document the evidence, and ensure that Milton's role would be undeniable. The shipment had arrived late last night, tucked in with a series of diplomatic vehicles marked for clearance. They'd tracked the convoy to a warehouse just outside D.C., where agents had seized several crates filled with military-grade weapons and smuggled drugs.

Now, the media was about to see it all—live on national television. Milton had no idea that the evidence, which he thought he could hide, was about to be aired for the world to see.

Garrett's phone buzzed quietly, and he checked the message. It was from Lancaster.

"I've hacked into Ortiz's secure channel. They know you're about to make your move. Milton will respond with force. Prepare for retaliation."

Garrett didn't need to hear any more. Lancaster's warning was enough. Ortiz had deep ties everywhere, and once they made their move, things were going to escalate fast.

At the front of the room, Senator Milton stepped up to the podium, his sharp suit and confident posture belying the fear he must have felt on the inside. The cameras clicked and flashed as he adjusted the microphone, a practiced smile on his face.

"Good afternoon," he began, his voice carrying effortlessly across the room. "I've called this press conference today to address the recent accusations made against my office and the rumors surrounding my so-called ties to international criminal organizations. These baseless allegations have no merit, and I am here to set the record straight."

Garrett's jaw clenched. He knew this moment would come. Milton would deny everything. He always did. But Garrett wasn't here for words—he was here for action.

As Milton continued his speech, a small group of reporters in the front row exchanged knowing glances. It was clear they were waiting for something. They had been briefed in advance. They had all seen the footage. The world was about to watch as their carefully laid trap unfolded.

Milton's words began to fade into background noise as Garrett's focus sharpened. Palmer turned to him, her expression tight. She had the remote in her hand—the device that would trigger the live broadcast of the video footage from the warehouse. It was a crucial moment, one that could shatter Milton's public image and send shockwaves through the political establishment.

Garrett gave her a small nod. She pressed the button.

Suddenly, the large screen behind Milton flickered to life, showing the footage of the cartel shipment being seized. There was no mistaking the weapons being unloaded, the crates marked with the unmistakable insignia of Ortiz's network. The footage then cut to one of the diplomatic vehicles, its cargo doors opening to reveal an array of crates packed tightly with drugs.

The room went silent.

Milton's eyes widened for a fraction of a second before he regained his composure, his face hardening. "This is a smear campaign!" he shouted, his voice laced with rage. "This footage is fake! This is all a setup!"

But the damage was already done. The reporters were shouting questions, demanding answers, the cameras capturing every moment of his frantic response. Garrett could almost feel the weight of the pressure mounting on Milton. He was a cornered animal, and there was no way out.

The media frenzy was immediate. News outlets began broadcasting the footage, and soon, Milton was being blasted across every network. He'd gone from being a respected senator to a public villain in a matter of minutes. It was chaos in the Capitol, and the stakes had never been higher. Garrett leaned back in his seat, satisfied with the moment. They had won. Or so he thought.

Palmer's phone buzzed. She glanced down at the screen and her expression changed. "Garrett, we have a problem," she said quietly, her voice tense. "Lancaster just sent a message. He's spotted a convoy approaching the Capitol building."

Garrett's blood ran cold. He knew exactly what that meant.

"Ortiz is making his move," Garrett muttered. "We've got to get out of here, now."

Before Palmer could respond, the ground shook beneath them as a loud explosion erupted from the streets below. Screams filled the air as chaos ensued. The glass windows of the conference hall rattled, and a plume of smoke rose from the area outside. Gunfire erupted, and the sound of shouting filled the hall as security scrambled to respond.

"Get down!" someone yelled, as the room erupted into a stampede. Guards rushed to secure the perimeter, but the attackers were already inside. A dozen men in tactical gear stormed the conference room, weapons drawn, their faces obscured by masks.

Garrett grabbed Palmer's arm and pulled her down behind a row of chairs, trying to stay low. The gunmen moved swiftly, methodical in their approach. They were here to kill—nothing more, nothing less.

Milton had dropped behind the podium, and Garrett could see the panic in his eyes as he realized the extent of the situation. The gunmen weren't here just for the press conference; they were here for him.

Garrett's mind raced. They needed to survive this. The exposure had worked, but now the real danger was just beginning. Ortiz's men were in the building, and they wouldn't stop until they had their target.

"Move!" Garrett hissed, pulling Palmer toward the exit. But it was too late. The door was already blocked, and more gunmen were spilling into the room.

The crowd screamed, ducking for cover as the attackers made their way to the front of the room. Milton was still crouched behind the podium, his eyes wide with fear, his hands shaking. His political career was crumbling in front of him, and Garrett knew the worst was still to come.

"Stay down!" Palmer shouted as they took cover behind a column.

Garrett's heart raced. The press conference had ended in chaos, and the world would be watching. But in that moment, all he could think about was survival.

The gunfire rang louder, closer, and the world seemed to blur as everything spiraled out of control.

Chapter 11: Blood on the Streets

The stench of burning rubber and gasoline lingered in the air as Garrett's car made its way down the winding dirt road leading to Kendrick's private compound in Colombia. The attack on the Capitol had left a trail of destruction, but Garrett had barely managed to stay one step ahead of those who would kill him to cover their tracks.

Now, the pressure was on. Kendrick, the arms dealer with a reputation for ruthlessness, had managed to remain in the shadows, pulling strings for Ortiz's private army. His compound, hidden deep in the Colombian jungle, was the last place Garrett wanted to be, but he had no choice. Kendrick was a key player in the operation, and if Garrett could get close enough, he might be able to expose the cartel's final weapon—an army built on military-grade weapons and vicious soldiers.

The sun was setting as Garrett pulled up to a large, iron gate. The compound loomed ahead, an imposing fortress of concrete and steel. Armed guards patrolled the perimeter, their eyes scanning the jungle for any sign of trouble. It was clear Kendrick was taking no chances, but Garrett had a plan.

He wasn't here to fight. Not yet, anyway. He had to get in, gather intelligence, and get out. Posing as a buyer for military equipment, he had convinced the cartel's middlemen that he could provide them with valuable contacts in the U.S. arms market. A risky move, but it was the only way to get in unnoticed.

The gate creaked open as a guard waved him through. Garrett's heart raced, his pulse pounding in his ears as the vehicle slowly rolled forward, passing by more guards and surveillance cameras. The compound was a labyrinth of buildings, each one fortified and heavily guarded. But in the middle of all the chaos, Garrett saw opportunity.

He parked the car and made his way toward the main building, where Kendrick was reportedly holed up. The man was notorious for being cautious—almost paranoid—but he also had an ego. Garrett would exploit that.

Inside, the atmosphere was tense. Men in fatigues milled about, cleaning weapons or talking in low voices. Garrett kept his head down, trying to blend in, his mind racing with the details of his plan. He had to make it to the meeting room, where Kendrick and his top lieutenants were rumored to meet with potential buyers. That was where he would find the information he needed.

As he walked through the corridors, he passed by a stack of crates, each one marked with Ortiz's insignia. The evidence was undeniable. Weapons—high-tech firearms, explosives, and equipment that would make any military force salivate. Garrett could feel the weight of what he was witnessing. If this was the arsenal that Ortiz's private army was using, the ramifications were enormous.

He finally reached the meeting room. The door was slightly ajar, and Garrett could hear voices inside. He pushed it open just enough to peer in. Kendrick was sitting at a large table with several other men, all of them hardened criminals with too much money and too much power. They were discussing the shipment—how much it would cost to get it past the Mexican border, which routes would be the most secure, and who they would sell it to.

The conversation was just as Garrett had anticipated. Kendrick's operation was massive, and Ortiz was at the center of it all. There were no details left to chance. The cartel had an army at its disposal, and Kendrick's weapons would ensure that they could control entire regions with brute force.

But it was what Kendrick said next that made Garrett's stomach churn.

"We'll need to move fast," Kendrick's gravelly voice echoed in the room. "Ortiz's people are getting impatient. They've got a big operation coming up, and this army will need to be in position before they strike."

Garrett's mind raced. What operation? And where?

He knew he had to get out of there before the situation escalated. But before he could back away, one of Kendrick's men noticed him lingering by the door. The guard's eyes narrowed, and Garrett's heart skipped a beat. He had been made.

"Hey!" the guard shouted, pointing directly at Garrett. "Who the hell are you?"

In an instant, everything changed. The room went silent, and all eyes were on Garrett. He had to think fast. Without hesitation, he lunged for the door and sprinted down the corridor, hearing the sound of heavy boots following close behind.

He knew the compound inside and out by now, but the chase had already begun. Garrett's heart pounded in his chest as he rounded a corner, moving through the building's maze-like hallways. The guards were relentless, and it was only a matter of time before they caught up with him.

He found a narrow side door leading outside and bolted through it, the humid air hitting him like a wall. But as he emerged into the compound's outer yard, he was confronted by another armed guard. Garrett didn't hesitate. He darted left, into the dense jungle that surrounded the compound. It was his only chance.

The dense foliage slowed him down, but it also gave him cover. He could hear the guards calling for backup as they swarmed the compound, but Garrett wasn't stopping. He pushed through the underbrush, his mind focused solely on escape.

Meanwhile, back in Mexico, Ramirez had been making his own moves. He had found a whistleblower within the Mexican Federal Police, a man who had been working with Ortiz for years. The information he provided was invaluable. Not only had he confirmed that Ortiz was planning a major smuggling operation using diplomatic immunity, but he also revealed that the cartel had a network of spies embedded in various law enforcement agencies across Mexico.

Ramirez was already on his way to meet the whistleblower in person, but the urgency of the situation had increased. Ortiz was pulling all the strings now, and the stakes had never been higher.

Garrett finally broke free from the compound's perimeter, disappearing into the jungle. He had to find a way to get back to the States, but it wasn't going to be easy. Kendrick and his men would be after him, and Ortiz's network was growing by the hour.

As Garrett made his way through the dense forest, he heard the unmistakable sound of a helicopter overhead. The search was already on.

In the distance, he could see the outline of a compound fence. Kendrick was closing in.

Garrett wasn't sure how long he could keep running. He had a target on his back now, and the walls were closing in faster than ever before.

But Kendrick was a threat that Garrett couldn't ignore. And he wasn't about to let him get away.

Chapter 12: The Cartel's Fortress

Garrett's head throbbed as he regained consciousness. His vision was blurry, and his limbs were stiff, bound tightly to a chair. The acrid smell of damp stone filled the air, and the faint sound of dripping water echoed in the cold, dimly lit room. He struggled against his restraints, but the ropes dug into his wrists, making any movement painful. The silence was oppressive, broken only by the occasional murmur from outside the room.

He had been taken by Kendrick's men, dragged through the jungle and into the mountains. Kendrick's pursuit had been relentless, and Garrett had never been more aware of his mortality. His capture had been inevitable—he had known too much, and Kendrick had made it clear that there would be no escape.

As his eyes adjusted to the darkness, Garrett realized he was inside a fortress. The walls were thick, constructed from stone that had clearly been in place for centuries, offering a sense of impregnable security. There were no windows, only small slits in the walls that allowed just enough light to cast shadows across the room. It was a place designed for one thing: control.

His heart raced as his mind raced through his options. He couldn't let this be the end. He had to escape, had to warn Lancaster, Palmer, Ramirez—everyone involved in bringing down Ortiz and the cartel. But first, he needed to figure out where he was, and what Ortiz wanted with him.

A door opened behind him, and the sound of heavy footsteps echoed in the hall. Garrett tensed, instinctively pulling against his bonds as the door creaked open.

Ortiz entered the room, flanked by Kendrick and two heavily armed guards. The cartel kingpin's cold eyes glinted with malice, his expression unreadable beneath his stubbled face. He looked like a man who had seen the world burn and had no intention of stopping the fire.

"Garrett," Ortiz said, his voice low and deliberate. "I've been expecting you."

Garrett remained silent, glaring at Ortiz. He refused to show any sign of weakness, even as the ropes threatened to cut off circulation. He could feel the sweat on his brow and the pounding of his heart, but he wasn't going to let Ortiz see him break.

"You've been digging into things you don't understand," Ortiz continued, stepping closer to Garrett. "The people you work for, the ones you trust—they have no idea what they're up against. What I'm doing here is bigger than anything they could ever imagine."

Garrett met Ortiz's gaze, not letting his fear show. "You're a monster. You'll never get away with this."

Ortiz chuckled softly, the sound like gravel being crushed beneath heavy boots. "You think I'm a monster? No, Garrett, I'm a visionary. I see the world for what it is—broken, corrupt, and ready for change. The people who run this world, they've grown fat and lazy, feeding off the suffering of others. But I'll show them something new. I'll show them power like they've never known."

He turned to Kendrick, nodding for the enforcer to step forward. Kendrick grabbed Garrett by the shoulders and roughly pushed him to the floor, kneeling beside him. Garrett's jaw clenched as the pain shot through his limbs, but he refused to let the man see him wince.

"You're a tool, Garrett," Ortiz said. "An obstacle. You've seen too much. But you're also resourceful, I'll give you that. You've come closer than anyone to understanding what we're doing here. But now that you're here, I'll tell you everything. It's time you understood the bigger picture."

Ortiz's cold smile faded, replaced by a grim determination. He stood up straight, crossing the room to a map on the wall. It was marked with various countries, including the United States, Mexico, and several key European nations. There were lines drawn across it, routes connecting different points, each one signifying a planned operation.

"This," Ortiz said, tapping a large red X on the map, "is where it all begins. We've built an empire over the past decade, quietly infiltrating governments, corporations, and entire industries. But now, it's time to strike. We're going to destabilize global markets. We're going to flood the world with bioengineered drugs—drugs that will not only control people, but give us leverage over governments. Governments will fall, Garrett. Economies will crumble. And those who survive will come crawling to us for protection."

Garrett's mind raced as he processed Ortiz's words. The scale of the plan was staggering. Bioengineered drugs? Political manipulation? He had been right—this wasn't just about smuggling or power. This was about reshaping the entire world.

Ortiz turned back to him, his eyes narrowing. "Do you understand now, Garrett? You thought you were playing a game of cat and mouse, but you were just a pawn. A small part of a much larger puzzle. I control everything now. And soon, I'll control the entire world."

Garrett's stomach churned at the thought. He had to stop Ortiz. But how?

Ortiz's gaze softened, almost as if he were savoring Garrett's helplessness. "Of course, it's too late for you. You've seen too much. But you'll be the first to see the power we're about to unleash on the world. And you'll die knowing you were the one who tried to stop it."

Garrett's blood ran cold as Ortiz walked toward Kendrick, speaking in a low voice. The enforcer's face was unreadable, but Garrett could see the coldness in his eyes. Kendrick was a man without empathy, a tool in Ortiz's twisted vision.

Ortiz turned back to Garrett, his smile widening. "I think it's time you learned your place."

He raised a hand, and Kendrick stepped forward, pulling a handgun from his belt. Garrett's breath caught in his throat as the enforcer aimed the weapon at his chest. The barrel was cold and unforgiving, and Garrett could feel his pulse quicken.

Before Ortiz could give the order, Garrett quickly shifted his position in the chair, discreetly pressing a hidden button on his watch. The signal had been sent.

Ortiz's hand dropped, his attention shifting to Kendrick. "Take care of it."

But before Kendrick could move, a faint sound—barely a whisper—came through Garrett's earpiece. Lancaster. He had received the transmission. Help was coming.

Garrett's heart pounded in his chest, but he knew he had to buy time. Ortiz was unpredictable, but Garrett wasn't going down without a fight. He had one chance to escape, one chance to stop this madness before it spread further.

Ortiz's cold eyes locked onto Garrett's once more, the smirk on his face never faltering. "You really think someone's coming to save you?"

Garrett's voice was steady, despite the fear gnawing at him. "It's not over, Ortiz. Not by a long shot."

Ortiz's smile faded, replaced by a look of cold fury. "Then you'll die believing in fairy tales."

He turned to Kendrick, nodding once more.

Kendrick's finger tightened on the trigger.

Chapter 13: An Unlikely Rescue

The sound of boots pounding against stone echoed through the dark hallways of Ortiz's compound. Lancaster and Ramirez moved swiftly, their movements deliberate and practiced. They had no time to waste—the rescue was their only chance. Garrett's life hung in the balance, and the evidence he'd gathered was critical. With Ortiz's plans threatening to destabilize the global order, there was no room for failure.

Ramirez, always the strategist, motioned for Lancaster to take the lead. They knew the layout of the compound, thanks to the intel they'd gathered. Ortiz's fortress was vast, its walls lined with armed guards, each more loyal than the last. But Lancaster was a seasoned veteran, and Ramirez knew he'd be able to hold his own. They had no other choice but to trust the plan.

They moved silently, slipping through the compound's narrow passageways, avoiding the heavily guarded open areas. The faint hum of electronic equipment echoed through the walls, a stark reminder of the high-tech operations that powered Ortiz's empire. But Lancaster and Ramirez were focused on one thing only—Garrett.

As they neared the central chamber where Garrett had been held, they heard the faint sound of voices, followed by a loud crash. Lancaster signaled for Ramirez to stay back and took point, crouching low as he approached the entrance to the room. He could see two guards standing watch outside the door, unaware of their impending danger.

With practiced efficiency, Lancaster raised his silenced pistol and took them down silently, his shots precise and deadly. The guards crumpled to the ground, their bodies hitting the floor with barely a sound. Ramirez moved in, his expression grim as he scanned the area.

"Clear," Lancaster whispered, his voice low but urgent.

They pushed through the door, and the scene before them was chaos. Garrett was still bound to the chair, but now there was blood on the floor. Ortiz's men had left their mark, and Garrett was barely conscious, his face bruised and battered from the brutal interrogation.

Lancaster rushed to Garrett's side, quickly cutting the ropes that bound him. "Come on, Garrett, we don't have much time."

Garrett's eyes fluttered open, his vision blurry as he tried to focus. "I thought you were dead," he muttered, his voice hoarse. "Get me out of here."

"Already on it," Ramirez replied, his voice sharp as he kept an eye on the door.

Garrett pushed himself to his feet, wobbling slightly as he leaned on Lancaster for support. The pain in his chest was almost unbearable, but he couldn't afford to show it. They had to keep moving.

"Where's the evidence?" Lancaster asked, his eyes scanning the room for anything useful.

Garrett pointed weakly to a small metal box on a nearby table. Inside, a hard drive containing everything Garrett had uncovered about Ortiz's global network. Lancaster grabbed it quickly, slipping it into a protective case.

"Let's go," Lancaster urged, pulling Garrett toward the door.

But just as they made it halfway across the room, the sound of boots echoed down the hallway. Ramirez raised his weapon, his eyes narrowing. "We're not alone."

Lancaster didn't hesitate. He pulled Garrett toward the nearest exit—a narrow stairwell that led to the roof. Ramirez took point, his weapon ready as he cleared the path ahead. The sounds of shouts grew louder behind them, but Lancaster knew they couldn't stop now.

The stairwell was steep, and the climb felt endless. Garrett's legs were weak, and every step sent sharp pangs of pain through his body. But he pushed through, knowing that the harder they fought, the closer they were to stopping Ortiz.

They reached the rooftop just as the first wave of guards burst through the stairwell door. Lancaster and Ramirez opened fire, their shots precise and deadly. The guards fell, but more were on the way. It wasn't long before the rooftop was filled with the sound of gunfire and shouts. Garrett had no idea how long they could hold out.

"Stay down!" Lancaster barked as he dove behind a nearby air vent, his weapon steady. Ramirez moved to a higher vantage point, firing from the rooftop's edge.

Garrett took cover behind a stack of crates, his heart pounding. He could hear the guards closing in, their footsteps heavy as they advanced. The pressure was mounting, and every second felt like an eternity. But then, as if on cue, Lancaster's earpiece crackled to life.

"Get out of there now," the voice said. It was Palmer. "The reinforcements are on the way, but you need to move fast."

Lancaster didn't hesitate. "Let's go. Now."

Ramirez and Lancaster laid down covering fire, their shots reverberating across the compound. Garrett followed them, his body still weak, but his determination unwavering. As they neared the edge of the rooftop, Lancaster pulled out a rope, tying one end to a nearby structure.

"Grab on," he ordered.

Ramirez went first, followed closely by Lancaster. Garrett hesitated for a moment, looking back at the compound. Ortiz would stop at nothing to protect his empire, and Garrett had no illusions about the danger they were in. But they had made it this far. He couldn't afford to fail now.

Taking a deep breath, Garrett grabbed the rope and swung down after them, the world blurring around him as they descended. The ground was just ahead—he could see the trees lining the edge of the compound. They were close.

The three of them hit the ground hard, rolling to absorb the impact. Lancaster was the first to regain his footing, quickly checking the surroundings. They had reached the outer perimeter of the compound, but the danger wasn't over yet.

"Move out," Lancaster said. "We've got the evidence. Now we need to get back to the safe house."

But as they sprinted toward the trees, a loud engine roared to life in the distance. Lancaster turned just in time to see a black SUV speeding toward them, kicking up dust in its wake.

Ortiz was already making his move. The convoy was on its way, and Garrett knew they had minutes—if that—to get out of range.

But it wasn't just the vehicle they had to worry about. As the SUV came into view, Garrett's heart sank. He could see Ortiz standing in the back, holding a small black box—something that looked far too important to ignore.

Ortiz's eyes locked with Garrett's, and in that moment, Garrett realized something crucial. Ortiz wasn't just running from them. He was taking something with him.

Ortiz was holding the key to his entire plan.

Chapter 14: A City Under Siege

The first sign of chaos came when the power went out. Across Washington, D.C., and several other major cities, the lights flickered and died, plunging entire districts into darkness. For a moment, there was only the eerie silence before the sound of sirens began to fill the air. It was only when the first explosions rocked the downtown core that Garrett realized what was happening. The cartel was making its move.

"Shit. They're hitting everywhere," Garrett muttered, his mind racing. Ortiz's operation was no longer a shadow in the background—it was in full force. Coordinated attacks across the globe, targeting political leaders, law enforcement agencies, anyone who might stand in the way of his empire. Garrett had warned them, but it felt like the world was unraveling faster than they could respond.

Garrett, Lancaster, and Ramirez had gathered at their temporary base—a secure location they'd set up in the wake of the attack on the Capitol. Palmer had arranged for encrypted communications with several global intelligence agencies, trying to assess the scope of Ortiz's offensive. The team worked quickly, analyzing the data they had recovered from the compound. Every file, every piece of intelligence was vital now.

They had already uncovered much of Ortiz's operation, but what had once seemed like a network of isolated, criminal dealings now appeared to be something far more dangerous. Ortiz wasn't just trying to control the drug trade—he was trying to control the world. Garrett couldn't shake the feeling that they were only scratching the surface.

"Look at this," Lancaster said, his voice tense as he sifted through the files. "This isn't just about smuggling. Ortiz is targeting key political figures across the globe. World leaders, military commanders... and law enforcement. They're planning a coup, and it's happening now."

Garrett leaned in, his eyes scanning the list of names that Lancaster had highlighted. It was a hit list—dozens of politicians, police chiefs, military generals. The names were scattered across countries, but there was a clear pattern. Key figures in positions of power were being targeted.

"We've got a summit of world leaders coming up next week," Palmer added, her voice crackling through the secure line. "Ortiz's people are likely planning an attack there. We need to get ahead of this—fast."

Ramirez, who had been pacing the room, stopped in his tracks. "The summit. If we don't stop them, we could lose more than just these leaders. This is about destabilizing entire governments."

Garrett nodded grimly. He could feel the weight of the situation pressing down on him. Every decision from here on out could mean the difference between saving millions of lives or losing everything. "We need to warn them. We need to shut down Ortiz's operations before he can strike."

The team worked through the night, piecing together a plan to prevent the attacks. Lancaster was already in contact with contacts in military intelligence, trying to track the movements of known cartel members. Palmer, with her network of operatives, began to put together a strategy to evacuate vulnerable targets. Meanwhile, Garrett focused on gathering more intel from the files, trying to uncover any weaknesses in Ortiz's operation.

It wasn't long before they discovered something even more unsettling.

"Garrett, you need to see this," Lancaster called from across the room.

Garrett crossed the room quickly, his heart pounding. Lancaster had opened an encrypted file, one that hadn't been flagged during their initial analysis. Inside, there were coordinates and names—likely connected to Ortiz's hit list. But there was something else.

"This... this can't be right," Garrett muttered, his fingers hovering over the screen. "This file is—it's a report. It's an internal memo."

"What do you mean?" Ramirez asked, stepping over to get a better look.

"Someone in our team is compromised," Garrett said, his voice tight. "The file's encrypted, but I'm sure of it. There's a report about an asset. It's not just anyone—it's someone we trust."

Lancaster stared at Garrett, his face a mask of disbelief. "Who?"

Garrett's eyes flicked to the screen. The name was buried within the encrypted document, but it was there. One of their own. Garrett's stomach churned. They had been betrayed. But who could it be? Palmer? Lancaster? Ramirez?

"I'll trace it back," Garrett said quickly, his mind working over the possibilities. "We need to find out who's behind this before it's too late."

But the more Garrett analyzed the file, the more questions arose. The report was too detailed—too specific. Whoever had written it knew exactly what they were doing. They had covered their tracks well. The betrayal ran deep, and it wasn't just about leaking information. It was about sabotage, about taking down their efforts from the inside.

Lancaster clenched his fists. "We can't afford to waste time. Whoever this is could bring the entire operation down."

The urgency was palpable. The stakes had always been high, but now they were even higher. If there was a mole within their ranks, it would be almost impossible to stop Ortiz's plan. They couldn't afford to be distracted by internal threats—not when the world was literally under siege.

Garrett didn't want to think about it, but the question gnawed at him: who could they trust?

Ramirez's voice broke the silence. "We need to secure the summit. That's priority number one. We can deal with the traitor after."

Garrett nodded, but he couldn't shake the feeling that this mole was watching them, waiting for the right moment to strike. He had no idea who it was or how deep the conspiracy went, but one thing was clear—this fight wasn't just about stopping a cartel. It was about surviving the storm of betrayal that was closing in on them from all sides.

They had to act fast.

As they made their preparations, every second felt like it could be their last. The city was in chaos. Bombings, assassinations, and the looming threat of political collapse created a sense of impending doom. But there was no turning back. Garrett had always known the risks, but now, as they scrambled to stop Ortiz's attack on the summit, everything felt personal.

And just as Garrett began to organize their next steps, his phone buzzed. It was an anonymous message, encrypted with a level of security only someone close to him could manage.

The message was simple, but the implications were clear:

"I know what you're planning. You won't stop him. He's already won."

Garrett's hand trembled as he read the message.

It was time to act—before it was too late.

Chapter 15: The Summit Gamble

The clock was ticking down to the international summit, and the team was racing against time. Garrett had never felt the weight of urgency like this before. The summit, a high-profile event bringing together leaders from across the globe, was a prime target for Ortiz's cartel. The stakes couldn't be higher—if they failed to stop the attack, it would trigger a global catastrophe.

"Garrett, we need to move," Ramirez said, his voice tense as he studied the briefing papers in front of him. "Ortiz won't wait for us to make our move. We have to be ready."

Garrett nodded, his mind running through the various scenarios. They knew Ortiz planned to use his aggression-enhancing drug on the summit attendees, injecting the guests with a bioengineered substance that would spark violence and chaos. Once chaos erupted, the cartel would sweep in, taking control of the summit's security and, from there, manipulating the political landscape to their advantage. The drug wasn't just a weapon—it was the key to triggering the collapse of governments.

Jennifer Palmer had arranged for a covert operation to secure the venue. They had reliable intel on the cartel's expected movements, but there was still so much unknown. The security at the summit was tight—foolproof, or so it seemed—but Garrett had seen enough to know that nothing was truly foolproof when it came to Ortiz's people. They had infiltrated every level of society, every agency, every government. There was always a way in.

And as Garrett looked over the room at his team, his thoughts kept returning to Palmer. The encrypted message, the sudden change in her behavior—it all pointed toward one thing: a mole. He had no concrete proof, but suspicion gnawed at him. Palmer had been helpful, yes. She had provided intel, arranged safe houses, set up covert meetings with operatives. But what if she was the one pulling the strings from the inside? What if she was working with Ortiz, feeding him information, compromising their efforts?

Garrett shoved the thought aside. There was no time for doubts, not now. They had a mission, and they had to focus. They had to stop the drug from reaching the summit.

Lancaster had been working furiously, putting together a plan to intercept the drug before it was distributed. "We know the delivery's coming in under the guise of diplomatic immunity," he said, tapping his laptop. "But we've got eyes on the shipment. I've arranged for a team to handle it before it gets to the venue."

"Good," Garrett replied. "But we can't afford a mistake. There's no room for error."

Ramirez was pacing near the window. "If we're wrong about the shipment, if we miss it—"

"We won't," Garrett interrupted. "But we also need to prepare for the worst. Ortiz's men will be everywhere. This is his big play. If we don't stop him here, it's over."

They were ready. Or so they hoped.

As the team moved out, Palmer stayed behind in the command center, coordinating with international contacts and monitoring communications. Garrett tried to push aside the nagging doubts about her involvement, but the thought lingered in the back of his mind.

The venue was on lockdown. Security was tight, with military personnel and law enforcement stationed throughout the building. Garrett and the team moved through the crowds, blending in with the other guests. Everything had to go according to plan. The delegates, from heads of state to diplomats, were unaware of the imminent danger lurking in the shadows. Garrett could see the tension in the eyes of some—nervous glances exchanged between leaders, whispers about the growing instability around the world. But no one knew the full extent of what Ortiz was about to unleash.

Hours passed. The summit began, and the team stayed on high alert. Garrett kept his eyes on the crowd, watching for any signs of trouble. There were the usual subtle movements, the discrete glances, but nothing that screamed danger. He checked his watch. Time was running out. The drug would be delivered soon. They had to stop it before it reached the leaders.

Palmer's voice crackled over the radio. "Garrett, the shipment's been intercepted. We've secured the drug. You're clear to proceed with the next phase."

"Roger that," Garrett replied, his heart pounding. They had a small window. Now, it was a matter of finding the people responsible for bringing the drug into the summit before it was too late.

But just as Garrett prepared to move, he felt a subtle shift in the air—a change in the atmosphere. It was almost imperceptible, but something felt off. He glanced around, scanning the crowd, and that's when he saw it. A man in a dark suit, a face unfamiliar to Garrett, was watching him from across the room. He wasn't looking at Garrett directly, but the man's gaze kept shifting between Garrett and his team.

"Shit," Garrett muttered under his breath. "We've got a tail."

Lancaster and Ramirez noticed it too. They were positioned strategically, observing the room, but now their eyes narrowed as they saw the same man move into position near the stage. The man was too calm, too composed for someone who should have been in the midst of a high-security event.

"It's him," Lancaster said, his voice sharp. "He's one of Ortiz's men. I'm sure of it."

Garrett's pulse quickened. If the cartel had a presence at the summit, it meant Ortiz had been ahead of them the entire time. They had been infiltrated. This was no longer just about stopping a shipment—it was about preventing an assassination, a political coup, a global crisis. They had to act fast.

The man slipped behind a column near the front of the room, and Garrett moved to follow, but as he did, something stopped him. A sudden shout erupted from the back of the room. People screamed as chaos erupted. Garrett turned just in time to see a flash of movement—someone in the crowd had gone down.

The assassin was already inside, hidden in plain sight, and now the clock was ticking even faster.

Chapter 16: A Line in the Sand

Garrett's heart raced as he moved through the crowd, trying to locate the assassin. He had only moments to prevent the chaos from spiraling completely out of control. The man in the dark suit—he wasn't just a bodyguard or a random delegate—he was trained, lethal, and he had a job to do. And Garrett was the target.

The screams from the back of the room had shifted the atmosphere entirely. People were running in every direction, trying to escape, while others scrambled to get a glimpse of what was going on. The security teams, caught off guard by the speed and precision of the attack, were only now beginning to react.

Garrett knew he had to act first. The man was still in sight, moving through the room with a sense of purpose, never losing his focus, never appearing to be flustered. It was clear he had been here before—this wasn't his first time at an event like this.

"Lancaster, Ramirez, we've got company," Garrett muttered under his breath as he quickly assessed his surroundings. "Stay sharp."

They were all trained for moments like this, but the scale of the situation was unprecedented. The cartel had reached into the very heart of the global political stage, and Garrett couldn't afford to let it succeed.

The assassin finally came into Garrett's sights again, and this time, there was no mistake. The man's gaze flicked briefly to Garrett's position. That was the tell Garrett had been waiting for. Without hesitation, Garrett darted toward him, moving quickly but quietly through the shifting crowd.

His footsteps were nearly silent, but the chaos around him only made it harder to keep the element of surprise. The assassin was moving with speed and precision, heading toward the back exit. He had an escape plan. Garrett had no intention of letting him get away.

He pushed through the mass of people, staying close to the assassin but careful not to give away his position too soon. The back doors of the summit hall were fast approaching. Once they were through there, Garrett knew the assassin would be in control—he had the tactical advantage outside.

Garrett pushed harder. His pulse quickened as he closed the distance. He could almost reach him, could almost grab him, when the man suddenly turned, moving with calculated precision. A sharp motion caught Garrett off guard, and in a flash, the assassin pulled a small knife from his jacket, aimed straight for Garrett's torso.

The knife missed, just barely, as Garrett dodged instinctively, but it was a near miss—too close for comfort. Without hesitation, Garrett brought his gun to bear, firing a single shot that found its mark. The assassin crumpled to the floor, the weapon slipping from his grasp as he collapsed.

Garrett exhaled slowly, his hand still tightly gripping his gun. The immediate threat was neutralized, but the larger danger was still in play. Ortiz's drug had already been released into the summit—he had seen delegates moving unsteadily, heard the first signs of agitation among the leaders. The drug was already working its terrible magic.

"Lancaster, Ramirez, check the delegates. We've got to stop this now before it spreads further." Garrett spoke quickly, his voice sharp with urgency.

As they secured the situation, Garrett's mind began to piece together the greater puzzle. Something didn't add up. The assassin had been at the summit for a reason, yes, but the broader operation seemed to be running smoothly—too smoothly. Garrett knew that Ortiz had planned for every contingency, but something felt off. Why hadn't they done more to hide the drug? Why hadn't they waited for a more opportune moment?

That's when it hit him: they had underestimated them. Ortiz had expected the drug to cause chaos, but now that it was out in the open, Garrett realized that they'd been on the back foot the whole time. The real threat wasn't just the drug—it was who was pulling the strings behind the scenes.

And that's when Garrett's thoughts turned to Palmer.

"Jennifer," he said, more to himself than anyone else. "She knew too much. She coordinated too many moves. How did she know exactly where the shipment would be?"

His mind raced. The pieces clicked into place. It had all been too easy—Palmer's quick access to the right people, her unfailing assistance at every turn. She'd arranged safe houses, facilitated meetings, and provided critical intel—but what if it had all been a part of Ortiz's larger plan?

"Garrett, you need to hear this," Ramirez's voice broke through his thoughts. "I've got something from the intel we pulled earlier. It's about Palmer."

Garrett's pulse quickened. "What do you mean?"

"I was digging into the records, following some leads. Palmer's connection to Ortiz wasn't what we thought. It was fabricated—someone fed her that information to manipulate you."

Garrett's stomach dropped. The weight of the realization hit him like a punch. Palmer—his trusted ally, his contact—had been playing him. But who had created the deception? Who had planted that false trail?

"I don't know, but it's clear," Ramirez continued, his voice steady but firm. "The mole is someone else. Someone we've trusted, someone we didn't see coming."

Garrett's thoughts raced as he reviewed their entire mission. There had been a constant shadow of betrayal hanging over their every move, and now it was clear: the real mole was closer than they'd thought.

The tension between the team had always been palpable, but now Garrett felt it weigh on him more than ever. As he turned, ready to confront the truth, a sudden, sharp pain shot through his neck.

He staggered, feeling his vision blur as the world around him seemed to tilt. His hand shot up to his throat, but it was too late. A small dart—barely visible—stuck from his skin.

"Garrett?" Ramirez's voice echoed faintly, but it felt like it was coming from a distance.

His knees buckled, and the world around him spun into darkness.

Chapter 17: Against the Clock

Garrett's vision blurred, and the world spun as the poison coursed through his veins, but he refused to stop. The bitter taste of the dart's venom was an agony he could feel in every breath, but he clenched his jaw and pushed forward. His hands shook, but his resolve remained unshaken. Ortiz's operation had to be stopped. No matter the cost.

"Garrett, you need to sit this one out," Lancaster's voice came through his earpiece, the concern thick in his words.

"No," Garrett growled, his voice hoarse. "I'm going. This ends tonight."

He staggered forward, the floor beneath his feet feeling unstable, his pulse hammering in his ears. Every step felt like a battle, every breath was a struggle against the poison that seemed intent on paralyzing him. But he knew they didn't have time. Ortiz's final stronghold was ahead, and the drug's production facilities were within reach. The mission had to be completed, and he would be damned if he let the cartel slip away again.

Ramirez moved beside him, steadying Garrett when he swayed, but he didn't say anything. His loyalty was clear. The team had been through hell together, and they weren't backing down now. Not when they were so close.

"Lancaster, I need your eyes on the ground," Garrett ordered, trying to ignore the dizziness pulling at his senses. "There's a trap waiting for us in there."

"Understood. I'm tracking your movement. Stay sharp. There's more than just the usual perimeter. Ortiz has layered defenses, and I'm not sure where they're all hidden."

Garrett didn't need to be told twice. He was already mentally prepared for the worst. Ortiz had always been one step ahead, and this stronghold, tucked away in the jungle, would be no different. It was heavily fortified, well-guarded, and brimming with traps designed for the unwary. But Garrett had been in worse. He had survived worse. And tonight, Ortiz wouldn't get the luxury of another escape.

They approached the entrance, a reinforced steel door that was locked down tight. Ramirez placed a charge on the door, carefully checking the wires as Garrett leaned against the wall, fighting to stay conscious. His vision was starting to go dark around the edges, his mind fogged by the poison, but he couldn't afford to pass out—not yet. Not while there was still work to be done.

The charge went off with a deafening crack, and the door flew open, revealing the compound's interior—a maze of long, dark corridors. The air smelled of chemicals, of the synthetic drugs that had poisoned entire cities. They had to get to the heart of this operation. Garrett motioned for Ramirez to take the lead.

"Lancaster," Garrett rasped, trying to focus, "set a path through. We don't have much time."

"I've got you. Watch your six."

The team moved quickly through the compound, the low hum of machinery echoing around them. Garrett's head felt heavy, and the tunnel vision was starting to settle in, but he pushed it back. They had to keep moving.

They were halfway through the labyrinthine complex when Lancaster's voice crackled through again. "There's a door up ahead. It's a control room, but it's locked down tight. I'm patching in now, but you'll need to cover me."

Garrett nodded and signaled Ramirez to take point. He could feel his muscles slowing, his limbs heavy, but still he moved, his gun at the ready. They reached the door Lancaster had mentioned, and the team huddled behind cover as Lancaster began his work remotely.

Seconds passed like minutes. Every sound seemed amplified—footsteps echoing, the hum of machinery, the pounding of his heart.

"Almost there..." Lancaster's voice was tight with concentration. Then a beep, followed by the hiss of the door unlocking.

"Go!" Garrett ordered, stepping forward into the control room.

Inside, rows of screens displayed the production facilities. The sight made Garrett's stomach churn. They were so close now—if they could destroy these operations, Ortiz's entire drug network would be crippled.

But just as he was about to step forward, a loud explosion rang out from the far side of the room. The walls shook, and the blinding light of the blast pushed them to the floor. Garrett hit the ground hard, his head slamming against the cold concrete. The poison was clouding his thoughts, making it difficult to keep his focus.

"Garrett!" Ramirez's voice was a shout as he crouched beside him, trying to lift him up. "You alright?"

Garrett blinked, his head spinning. The blast had disoriented him, and now the weight of the poison threatened to take over. But through the haze, he saw Ramirez looking at him, waiting for a sign.

"Go," Garrett managed to rasp. "I'll hold them off."

Ramirez hesitated for only a moment before nodding sharply. He got to his feet, turning to follow Lancaster's orders.

Garrett, still struggling to stay conscious, drew his weapon. He couldn't let this be the moment they failed. Ortiz was too close to victory. Garrett's mind worked furiously through the options, all while his body fought against him.

Gunfire erupted from the other side of the compound. There was no time to lose.

Lancaster's voice cut through his thoughts. "Garrett, get out of there now. Kendrick's on the move."

Before Garrett could react, he heard the distinct sound of heavy boots coming closer. His heart raced. Kendrick. The arms dealer was here. He had been one step behind them this entire time, and now he was coming for them.

"Stay down," Ramirez called over his shoulder, disappearing into the smoke and chaos.

Garrett couldn't stay on the floor. He forced himself to his feet, gripping his weapon, and moving toward the sound of Kendrick's men. They weren't going to get away. Not after everything they had done to get this far.

A flash of movement caught his eye. Kendrick appeared in the doorway, flanked by two of his men. The guns came up, but Garrett was faster. He fired first, taking down one of Kendrick's guards, but the other returned fire.

The room filled with the deafening sound of gunfire. Garrett's instincts kicked in, but his movements were sluggish. The poison was taking its toll.

Through the haze of gunfire, Garrett heard the sound of retreating footsteps. Kendrick was pulling back.

"Ortiz is getting away!" Lancaster's voice rang out over the comms.

Garrett's blood ran cold. Ortiz had one final escape route—hidden beneath the compound. And he was taking it.

Without hesitation, Garrett sprinted forward, despite the agony in his chest and the dizziness that threatened to overwhelm him. He could barely focus, but he knew they couldn't afford to let Ortiz slip through their fingers.

The chase was on, and Garrett wasn't about to let it end like this.

Chapter 18: Collapsing Empire

The mission had been successful, but Garrett couldn't shake the feeling that they were only scratching the surface. They had hit Ortiz where it hurt—his drug production, his financial network, his underground empire of influence—but it wasn't enough. Not yet. Ortiz was still out there, a shadow in the background, just beyond their reach. The man had a way of disappearing, of slipping through their fingers like sand.

Garrett's team had taken down a massive portion of Ortiz's operation. Ramirez had secured the financial records that tied Ortiz to international criminal syndicates and corrupt officials. Lancaster had worked tirelessly to disable the bioengineered drug production facilities that were threatening to flood the world. Every piece of the infrastructure they took down felt like a victory, but it didn't feel like the end.

As they moved through the compound, Garrett's mind raced. He had seen what Ortiz was capable of. He knew the depths of the man's cruelty, and he couldn't shake the image of the drug-induced chaos the cartel had unleashed across the world. The global markets were on the verge of collapse, and Ortiz had an uncanny ability to stay a step ahead.

"Garrett, check this out," Ramirez's voice pulled him back from his thoughts.

Garrett turned to find Ramirez huddled over a series of screens, his fingers flying over the keys as he worked to decrypt more of the financial documents they had seized. The data was overwhelming, but they were making progress.

"This is bigger than we thought," Ramirez continued, his tone grim. "There's a pattern to his dealings. The drug production was only part of the equation. Ortiz has been positioning himself to launch a massive cyberattack. He's got a network of hackers set up to destabilize global markets. If this goes off, it'll be chaos."

Garrett stepped closer, his eyes scanning the documents Ramirez was pulling up. It didn't take long to see the magnitude of what they were facing. A cyberattack, launched from multiple points around the globe, targeting the financial systems of some of the world's largest economies. It wasn't just a criminal enterprise anymore. This was a power grab on a global scale.

"How much time do we have?" Garrett asked, his voice low.

"Not much," Ramirez replied, shaking his head. "This is a ticking time bomb. It could be any moment now. If we don't shut this down, Ortiz will not only have the money and power he needs, but he'll collapse the world's financial systems and watch everything burn."

Garrett clenched his jaw. They had been too slow. Too cautious. The urgency hit him like a punch to the gut. Ortiz wasn't just a drug kingpin anymore. He was a puppet master, pulling the strings on a global scale. If they didn't act now, there would be no fixing the damage.

"We need to find Ortiz," Garrett said, his voice hardening. "If he's behind this cyberattack, we need to stop him before he pulls the trigger."

"Already on it," Lancaster's voice crackled through the comms. "I'm tracking every trace of his movements. There's a secure location, some kind of safehouse, where the cyberattack is being initiated. I'm sending you the coordinates now."

Garrett nodded and grabbed his gear. They didn't have time to waste. The team moved quickly, navigating the labyrinth of tunnels beneath Ortiz's compound. There was no more hesitation, no more second-guessing. It was time to end this.

As they reached the surface, the oppressive heat of the jungle hit them. The air was thick with humidity, and Garrett's every breath felt like he was inhaling fire. But it didn't matter. They had a target now. They had a place to go, and Ortiz was there, hiding in the shadows.

The ride to the safehouse was tense. Garrett's mind was racing, but he kept his thoughts focused on the task at hand. The world was on the brink, and they couldn't afford to make mistakes. They had to get to Ortiz, shut down his operation, and end the threat before it was too late.

As they approached the safehouse, Lancaster's voice came through again, urgent and steady. "The place is heavily fortified. Ortiz has a private army, and it's well-guarded. I can't get any closer without drawing attention."

"We'll handle it," Garrett responded, his grip tightening around his weapon. "You stay back and provide cover. We'll get in, find Ortiz, and stop the cyberattack."

The team moved silently through the dense jungle, their steps quick and calculated. They knew the risks. They knew the enemies they would face. But nothing mattered except stopping Ortiz.

They reached the safehouse perimeter and began their breach. Ramirez worked the explosives, and within minutes, the doors were blown wide open. They stormed in, guns up, eyes scanning every corner for threats. The building was eerily quiet, save for the distant hum of machinery. They were close now. Garrett could feel it.

"Garrett, look at this," Ramirez called, his voice tense.

Garrett turned to find Ramirez standing in front of a set of large monitors, each one displaying a live feed of various global financial markets. The attack was already underway. Stock markets were plummeting. Bank systems were being breached. It was chaos, and it was spreading quickly.

"Shut it down," Garrett ordered, his voice sharp.

But Ramirez was already on it, his fingers flying over the keyboard as he worked to disable the systems. The countdown clock on the screen showed just how little time they had left. Seconds. The threat was right in front of them.

"I can't stop it all," Ramirez said, his voice tinged with frustration. "But I can slow it down. We need to find Ortiz."

Garrett nodded, his eyes scanning the room. There were no signs of Ortiz yet, but he knew the man wouldn't go down without a fight.

As they moved deeper into the compound, Garrett felt his phone vibrate in his pocket. He pulled it out, expecting another message from Lancaster. Instead, it was a call. An unknown number.

He answered it without hesitation.

"Garrett," Ortiz's voice was smooth, almost amused. "I see you've been busy. You've done well to dismantle my little operation, but you're too late. The world is already on fire. You can't stop it now."

Garrett's blood ran cold. He could hear the smugness in Ortiz's tone, the confidence of a man who thought he had already won.

"What do you want?" Garrett growled, keeping his voice steady.

"I want you to know that it's all over. Your efforts were futile. My cyberattack is already in motion, and nothing you do will change that. It's only a matter of time before the world crumbles under the weight of my empire. You can try to stop me, but you'll fail. Just like everyone else."

Ortiz's laughter echoed in Garrett's ear, sending a chill down his spine.

"Here's the ultimatum," Ortiz continued, his tone turning icy. "You can either step away now and watch the world burn, or you can keep fighting and die with the rest of them. The choice is yours."

The line went dead.

Garrett stood frozen, the phone still pressed to his ear. The taunt echoed in his mind. Ortiz had planned this from the start. He had never intended to be caught.

The world was on the brink, and Garrett had just been handed an ultimatum he couldn't ignore.

Chapter 19: The Last Bargain

The air was thick with tension, the silence almost suffocating as Garrett stood in front of Ortiz. The room around them, dimly lit and lined with monitors showing the chaos unfolding in real time, felt like a tomb. The ticking of a clock somewhere in the background echoed in Garrett's mind, reminding him of the limited time they had left.

Ortiz was calm, almost too calm. His hands were folded on the table in front of him, his gaze never wavering from Garrett. There was no sign of fear or urgency in his expression—just the quiet confidence of a man who had already won.

"You're a persistent one, Garrett," Ortiz said, his voice smooth and almost admiring. "I'll give you that. But you're not thinking clearly. You can't win this fight. Not anymore."

Garrett didn't respond immediately. He kept his posture tense, his eyes scanning Ortiz for any hint of weakness, but it was clear that the man before him was no ordinary criminal. He was a mastermind, a puppet master pulling strings on a global scale. And Garrett was just one piece in his twisted game.

Ortiz leaned back in his chair, his smile widening as he spoke again. "You've done your job well, I'll admit. You've managed to disrupt my operations. But all of it—everything you've done, all the bloodshed and the loss—it's just a part of the plan. You see, Garrett, there's more at stake here than just drugs or money."

Garrett's heart rate quickened. He had a feeling Ortiz was about to reveal something that would change everything. "What are you talking about?"

Ortiz's smile faded, replaced by a cold, calculated look. "The world has betrayed me, Garrett. Betrayed my family. The governments, the power players—they took everything from us. They took my family, my legacy. And now, they're going to pay for it. I've been planning this for years. Every move I've made, every operation, every scheme—it's been about revenge."

Garrett felt a flicker of doubt. He had known Ortiz was ruthless, but this? A vendetta on such a grand scale? It was almost too much to comprehend. He had always believed the cartel kingpin was about power, money, and influence. But this—this was personal.

"You're insane," Garrett spat, his voice laced with disgust. "You're willing to destroy the entire world for revenge? To throw everything into chaos because of a personal grudge?"

Ortiz's eyes darkened, his voice dropping to a cold whisper. "You don't understand. You don't know what it's like to lose everything. To have your family, your home, your future ripped away by corrupt officials. They made me who I am. And now I'm going to make them pay."

Garrett felt a surge of anger, but he kept his emotions in check. He had faced worse odds before, and he wasn't about to let this man manipulate him with his sob story.

"I didn't come here to listen to you talk about your vendetta," Garrett said, his voice hardening. "I came to stop you."

Ortiz nodded slowly, his fingers tapping against the edge of the table. "I expected nothing less. But perhaps, Garrett, you're not as different from me as you think. Maybe you, too, have lost something. Maybe you've felt the sting of betrayal, the weight of a broken world."

Garrett clenched his fists. "I'm nothing like you."

Ortiz's expression shifted, and for a moment, there was a flicker of something almost like pity in his eyes. "I can offer you a way out," he said, his tone suddenly more cordial. "Walk away. Leave this all behind. You've fought hard, and I respect that. But you don't have to die here today. You don't have to be part of this."

The offer hung in the air between them, tempting in its simplicity. Garrett felt a rush of conflicting emotions—fear, anger, disbelief—but above all, the clarity that came with the choice Ortiz was presenting.

"All you have to do is let go. Let me finish what I started, and you can walk away from all of this. Your team, your mission, your life—it can all be yours again, Garrett. No more fighting. No more bloodshed. Just... peace."

Garrett's mind raced. He had seen too much to even entertain the idea of accepting Ortiz's offer. The world was on the brink of collapse, and this man, who had brought it all to the edge of destruction, was offering him a way out? Garrett wasn't naive enough to believe that walking away would solve anything. It would only allow Ortiz to continue his path of destruction unopposed.

"I won't walk away," Garrett said, his voice low and resolute. "You've crossed a line, Ortiz. There's no going back for you now. You're going to pay for what you've done."

Ortiz's expression hardened, and the room seemed to grow colder. He stood up slowly, his movements deliberate, almost as if savoring the moment. "I didn't want to do this, Garrett," he said, his voice now dangerously calm. "But you leave me no choice."

Before Garrett could react, Ortiz pressed a button on the console in front of him. The sound of mechanical locks releasing echoed through the room, and a series of screens lit up, each showing a countdown. It was the cyberattack—activated, and there was no stopping it now.

The world's financial systems were under assault, and Ortiz was about to bring it all crashing down.

Garrett's heart skipped a beat as he realized the full scale of what was happening. The countdown was rapidly approaching zero. If the attack succeeded, entire economies would collapse in a matter of hours. It would be anarchy. And Garrett would be powerless to stop it in time.

Ortiz's voice cut through the air, filled with cold satisfaction. "It's already done, Garrett. The attack is in motion. You can't stop it now. You can try, but it's too late."

Garrett's mind raced. He had to make a choice—now. The options were limited. His team was still in danger, the global economy was on the brink, and Ortiz had just pushed the world one step closer to catastrophe.

But Garrett wasn't thinking about the world at that moment. He wasn't thinking about the countless lives in danger, the destruction that was coming. All he could focus on was the cold smirk on Ortiz's face, the finality in his words.

And then, Ortiz offered him one last choice.

"You can stop this, Garrett. You can end it right now. All you have to do is agree to my terms. Join me. And I'll call off the attack."

Garrett stood frozen, his mind swirling with every possible outcome. The weight of the world pressed down on him. He knew what he had to do.

But as he stood there, the countdown continued, relentless, and the choice loomed larger than ever before.

Chapter 20: The Chain Breaks

Garrett's pulse was racing, his hand gripping the edge of the console. He could feel the weight of the decision pressing down on him, suffocating him. The countdown on the screen ticked down relentlessly. Each second felt like a lifetime. Ortiz stood there, watching him with a twisted smile, his fingers drumming on the armrest of his chair.

"Time's almost up, Garrett," Ortiz said, his voice a smooth whisper. "One choice, one simple choice, and you can save everything."

Garrett's mind was a whirlwind, his body tense with the strain of knowing that in the next few seconds, the world could either be thrown into chaos or saved, at the cost of everything he had worked for. Ortiz's cyberattack was already in motion. He had no time to waste, no time to chase Ortiz down.

Ortiz had been right all along. There was no way to stop the cyberattack and capture him. The systems were already compromised. The attack was set in motion, and the world's financial markets were about to collapse. The lives of millions would be shattered.

But Garrett knew one thing: stopping the cyberattack would save them all, even if it meant letting the mastermind escape.

He could hear Lancaster's voice in his ear, distant but urgent. "Garrett, don't do this. We need Ortiz. If you stop the attack now, he's going to get away."

But Garrett didn't care. The mission, the hunt—everything else—could wait. Saving those lives meant more than taking down one man, no matter how dangerous. His hand hovered over the console, fingers trembling as the seconds slipped away.

Ortiz's voice broke through his thoughts. "You're not really going to let them all die, are you?" he asked, the mockery in his tone evident. "You're going to sacrifice millions just to stop me? To stop this?"

Garrett's fingers tightened. There was no choice. He slammed his hand down on the button, stopping the countdown with only seconds to spare. The monitors around him flickered, and for a brief moment, he thought it was a mistake—thought it hadn't worked.

Then, the room was silent. The threat of global chaos was gone. He had done it. The cyberattack was disabled, the global markets saved from total collapse. But at what cost?

Ortiz was already moving. Garrett knew it was too late to catch him. He watched as the cartel leader stepped back into the shadows of the room, the smug grin never leaving his face. The air in the room felt colder now, filled with the bitter taste of defeat.

"Smart move, Garrett," Ortiz said, his voice dripping with sarcasm. "You saved the world. But it's too late to stop me."

Before Garrett could react, Ortiz was gone—disappearing into the shadows with a speed and precision that spoke to the depths of his resources.

Garrett stood motionless, his heart pounding in his chest, the weight of his decision settling over him. He had stopped the attack. He had saved millions of lives. But he had also let the most dangerous criminal in the world slip away once again.

He had no time to dwell on it. The team would be waiting. He had to report back, face the consequences, and figure out what came next.

Lancaster's voice broke through his earpiece once more, but this time, it held no anger, no blame. "Good job, Garrett. You did the right thing. The world's still here because of you."

Garrett didn't answer. He couldn't. His mind was still locked on the fact that Ortiz had escaped, that the mastermind behind it all had slipped through his fingers yet again. But Lancaster was right in some ways. He had saved millions of lives. That had to count for something.

Back at their headquarters, the team was waiting. Ramirez was standing by the monitors, the weight of the mission heavy on his shoulders. He met Garrett's gaze when he walked in, his expression somber but understanding.

"You did what you had to do," Ramirez said quietly. "Ortiz is still out there, but you stopped him from bringing the world to its knees. That's what matters."

Garrett nodded but didn't respond. Ramirez was right, but the victory felt hollow. Ortiz was still out there, plotting his next move, and Garrett knew the man wouldn't rest until he had brought the world to its knees once and for all.

Lancaster was the next to speak, her voice steady and calm. "We'll get him. We always do. You didn't lose, Garrett. You just made a choice. And we'll keep fighting, keep moving forward. We won't stop until he's taken down."

Garrett finally allowed himself a deep breath. The team was still intact. They were still united. And they had a mission to finish.

"We'll find him," Garrett said, his voice low and determined. "But we need to rebuild first. Get our heads on straight."

Ramirez nodded, the weight of their shared experience evident in his expression. "My family's been through a lot. But we'll rebuild. We've got each other."

Garrett felt a flicker of hope. Maybe it wasn't all lost. The fight wasn't over. The battle had shifted, but it wasn't done. Ortiz was still a threat, but Garrett would make sure that the cartel leader didn't win.

As they stood there, the distant sounds of the city outside their window reminded them that life would go on. But in the back of Garrett's mind, he knew the truth: Ortiz hadn't been defeated. He was just waiting for the right moment to strike again.

Later that evening, as Garrett sat alone in his office, the flicker of a news report caught his attention on the screen in front of him. It was a breaking story about the recent events—the cyberattack, the cartel, and the disruption in the global markets. The newscaster was speaking about the rising threat of organized crime, the aftermath of the operation.

But then something in the report caught Garrett's eye. There, in the background of a report on Ortiz's cartel, a familiar face flashed briefly on the screen. The face was partially obscured, but Garrett knew the look. He had seen it before.

Ortiz. Or rather, someone who resembled him. Someone who was working under a new identity.

Garrett's stomach sank as he realized the truth. Ortiz had already moved on, already set the stage for his next move. The chain wasn't broken. It was just invisible, hidden in plain sight.

Ortiz's empire wasn't finished. It had only begun to shift.

Did you love *The Power of Invisible Chains : A Conspiracy, Crime & Political Thriller*? Then you should read *Sin's Fraternity A Psychological Thriller*[1] by Marcelo Palacios!

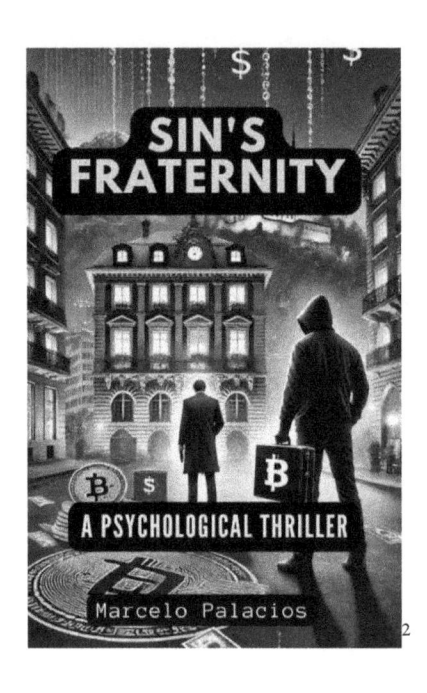

In the vibrant city of Geneva, an exclusive group known as "Sin's Fraternity" orchestrates an international money laundering ring that defies all laws. When private investigator Lucas Ferrer and cryptography expert Diana Montero discover the clues to this sinister club, they are plunged into a world of intrigue and danger.As they unravel a complex web of corruption, betrayal and tax evasion, Lucas and Diana face constant threats and unexpected double-crosses. Their quest for justice takes them from luxurious mansions in the Swiss Alps to dark alleys of the city, revealing a secret network of powerful criminals willing to do anything to protect their secrets.With intense storytelling and unexpected twists, "Sin's Fraternity" is a mystery and crime thriller that keeps readers on the edge of their seats. Get ready for a reading experience filled with suspense, tension and shocking revelations. Will Lucas and Diana succeed in dismantling

---

1. https://books2read.com/u/3yXJXJ

2. https://books2read.com/u/3yXJXJ

the network before it is too late, or will they fall into the deadly trap of the sinners? Find out in this exciting novel where every secret could be the last.

Also by Marcelo Palacios

El Club de los Pecados Un Thriller Psicológico
La Habitación Resonante Un Thriller Psicológico
Mentiras en Código Un Thriller Político
The Political Lies A Political Thriller
Sin's Fraternity A Psychological Thriller
El Cuarto de los Ecos Un Thriller Psicologico lleno de Suspenso
The Room of Echoes A Psychological Thriller Full of Suspense
El Espejo Perturbador Un Thriller Psicologico
The Disturbing Mirror A Psychological Thriller
Luces Apagadas en la Ciudad Brillante Un Thriller Psicológico,Crimen y Policial
Lights Out in the Shining City A Psychological, Crime and Police Thriller
Under the Cloak of Horror A Criminal Psychological Thriller full of Abuse, Corruption, Mystery, Suspense and Adventure
The Housemaid's Shadow A Psychological Thriller
Unraveling Marriage, Unraveling Divorce A Domestic Thriller
The Power of Invisible Chains : A Conspiracy, Crime & Political Thriller